Felicity Savage

BLACK WEDDING
AND
FIVE MORE FUNERALS

a collection of short stories

KNIGHTS
HILL

FIRST KNIGHTS HILL PUBLISHING EDITION, JUNE 2011

Knights Hill Publishing ISBN: 978-1-937396-04-6

www.knightshillpublishing.com

Printed in the United States of America

BLACK WEDDING
AND
FIVE MORE FUNERALS

BLACK WEDDING

To Jess's secret delight, the English weather forecast had proved inaccurate. Rain bucketed down on the grounds of Kilbore House, on the angular walks and the stone urns full of carnations dyed purple and yellow which had been cunningly insinuated amidst the native ferns for the occasion. The wedding guests were directed indoors.

Jess, arriving from the Plymouth registry office in a Land Rover full of Garnett cousins, stood at the back of the ballroom and watched it fill up with suits and taffeta froth. Posh, she thought, savoring the word, laughing a little at herself. *Rawther* posh, dahling!

When Jess and Sophie had lived together in college, Sophie had scorned any function that required her to wear heels. Now she was getting married in Veronica Wang.

But in one respect, perhaps, Sophie had not changed at all.

Jess had gotten her first look at the groom at the registry office. Tall and leonine with a head of parti-bleached straw, tanned like a mountaineer, Dhaka Huddingsley had exceeded Jess's expectations. She had feared that Sophie was about to marry some awful dweeb with a surgically attached briefcase. A barrister Dhaka might be; a dweeb he clearly was not. And it was not the PR professional with gleaming hair, now proceeding into the ballroom under full satin sail, who had fallen in love with him (Jess thought, clapping her hands sore); it was the scruffy little English hippie who'd spent four years getting stoned with Jess at Bennington and travelling on all-night magic carpet rides through the archipelagic possibilities of the future, shooting emotional rapids as deep as the gulfs between the stars. Jess had once been scared for Sophie. Now she felt proud of her.

A woman minister conducted the ceremony on the dais. ("What a pram-face," muttered a man near Jess, startling her into a giggle.) A Huddingsley uncle and Sophie's mother contributed readings from e.e. cummings and Tennyson. Beneath an arch of braided flowers Sophie and Dhaka took their vows. Camera flashes hailed on them, the wedding photographer did the splits, and Jess, having snapped her own pictures, surreptitiously hiked up her hose.

Three Things About Tom Fairweather (Only Two of Which are True)

Tom cannot swim

Tom once met the late General Ceaucescu of Roumania

Tom is a murderer

"Oh, now I get it," Jess said. She looked around the table. A heavy crossfire of conversation had already started up, the woman on Jess's right lobbing grenades of laughter. "Who's Tom Fairweather?"

"I am, I'm afraid," said the man on her left. "Friend of the family. The Garnetts, that is." His fine, straight blond hair was receding slightly from his temples. He gave an impression of solidity and calm. He glanced at the obverse of his own placecard. "Would you be Jessica Brentwood? Sophie's friend from university?"

"Yeah, but everyone calls me Jess. Well, then, we've got each other's."

"Hmm, well, in the spirit of the game, I'll guess it's untrue that you... once won a trophy for Jello wrestling."

Jess laughed. "No! That's actually one of the true things! It was on spring break ten years ago... totally out of character. I mean, I've never even been back to Florida since."

"Jello," Tom mused. "What we call jelly."

"And for us, the stuff you spread on your toast is jelly."

"Don't you eat it with peanut butter?"

"Not me. I'm actually allergic to peanuts." With her fork Jess touched the brick of quivering green-spotted substance framed amidst the leaves and shrimp of her appetizer. "Jelly."

"I think that's actually a sort of seaweed mousse," Tom said. Jess tasted it and made a face: so-so. He smiled. "OK, now I'm genuinely curious. Is it untrue that you're a teacher?"

"Two strikes and you're out," Jess crowed. "I'm a special education teacher in the New York public school system." She rolled her eyes. "Obviously, I do it for love."

"You certainly wouldn't do it for the money," Tom agreed.

"No, it's a total scandal... anyway. Don't get me started on politics. No, but I do love it: my kids are great. The smallest victory makes such a difference to them. Actually, they teach me as much as I teach them, you know? The importance of the little things in life." Jess smiled, and thought: Stop it, he's not interested. Around English people, with the great exception of Sophie, she always seemed to talk more about herself than she meant to. Their reserve and natural politeness drew her out, helplessly. "So tell me about meeting Ceaucescu," she said.

"I was only about eight. My father was a diplomat... no, quite boring, really. One international school is much the same as another. Anyway, there was a Christmas party at the palace. They used to invite all the children of the ambassadors and high-level apparatchiks; there was a Santa with amazing presents. But was I grateful? Not a bit. I was introduced to the General and I looked up at him – he was remarkably ugly, he looked as if he wasn't human at all, really – and I said, 'My mother says you're a tyrant.'" Tom burst into laughter. Jess joined in.

"No way! What did he say?"

"I can't remember; I think I was hustled off the scene in a hurry." Tom's blue eyes shone nostalgically. "Funnily enough, my parents divorced the year after that."

"Oh. I'm sorry."

"And a few years after *that*, of course, the General was deadibones."

"Yes, and good riddance," Jess said. "I remember the pictures in the papers."

They ate in silence for a few minutes. The appetizers had been replaced by plates of lamb, basmati rice, and a selection of vaguely Middle Eastern salads. At the head table, Sophie glowed beside Dhaka, and Jess wondered when she would get to catch up with her properly. She had only flown in this morning, on the red-eye from JFK. *Deadibones...* English slang was such a rich trove of oddities, like an antique shop where the mangles and fire irons walked and talked. The laughing-grenade woman said to her other seatmate, "So I told Arthur, I know they're very nice people, but I simply can't have them in our home again..."

"What I've been wondering," Jess said, "is, what kind of parents name their child after the capital of Bangladesh?"

At exactly the same time, Tom said, "So I'm assuming it's not true that you're married?"

They both laughed. Jess said, "No, I'm divorced, actually." Tom gave her what she thought of as The Look, eyes widening in a combination of surprise and belated understanding. Jess had once reveled in her status as a divorcee. Parents, for instance, talked freely and confidentially to her, as they did not talk to her never-married and presumably less worldly-wise colleagues. But more recently she felt as if

4

she had been sprayed with a coat of faux-aging patina, her bloom prematurely tarnished. Almost crossly, she said, "It was years ago. I was married at twenty-one, divorced at twenty-three... just a normal bad relationship. Except that we happened to tie the knot, so then we had to untie it again."

"A normal bad relationship," Tom said. "Is there any other kind?"

"Is that the voice of experience I hear?"

"No, no, just my usual—" He made a deprecating gesture. "Pop psychology."

At the head table a glass chimed. The Huddingsley uncle rose, a weathered yeti in a bowtie. Did Dhaka have no other family here? Jess could not see anyone who looked as if they might have named their child after the capital of Bangladesh, no greying hippies or intellectuals in Birkenstocks. "My nephew has a history of making mistakes," blared the uncle. "Especially in love. When he introduced me to Sophie – this beautiful, accomplished young woman – I knew he'd done it again. 'Dhaka,' I demanded, 'why haven't you married her already?'"

Laughter rolled through the room.

"It *was* a whirlwind romance, though," Jess whispered to Tom. "I hadn't heard from her in six months – she'd said nothing about a boyfriend – and then suddenly it was like, 'I've met The One and we're getting married next month!' I had to basically go on my knees to get the time off."

Tom's eyes slewed around to her. "I believe it runs in the family."

"Whirlwind romances?"

"No – I suppose a sort of self-sufficiency... it can feel like indifference. Rather terrifying really. They're very rooted here in South Devon, you know."

Eight miles from Plymouth, the Garnett family home lay on and virtually across a narrow lane that ran down to a stony cove. Today the rain had kept away the tourists who were known to brazenly park their cars in the front yard. The trees stooped low, dripping.

Additions jutted out of the house at odd angles, trikes and toy trucks cluttered the hall, and in the conservatory the families and friends of the newlyweds mingled amidst aloes and trays of seedlings while the rain pounded ceaselessly above their heads. Sophie's mother, Louise, came and talked to Jess, trailing a toddler. From Sophie, Jess had the impression that Louise entertained a neverending succession of men friends and had never stopped having babies, although this one was more likely to be a grandchild at Louise's age, she thought.

Still pink and blonde, if worn thinner than the last time they had met, Louise pressed Jess's arm with a cold hand. "Thank you for coming, Jess. You'll be staying with us, of course. Has anyone shown you where you'll be sleeping?"

"Not yet," said Jess, stifling a jetlagged yawn. "I'm having so much fun." This was one of those lies that made her fear she was turning into her own mother. "Sophie looks absolutely incredible." Wistfully, she gazed across the conservatory at Sophie, who had managed to give her one brief hug before being surrounded by her London-based bridesmaids and their loud escorts.

Tom Fairweather caught her eye and jerked his head. She rose and went to stand beside him on the fringe of the group, feeling slightly awkward.

"I'm not advocating social Darwinism," Dhaka said. His eyes were as pink as the champagne at lunch, a left-over bottle of which he gripped by the neck. "I'm only saying people have got to be held accountable to their communities. Christ, we can't leave the law in the hands of the *lawyers!*"

"You'd know," shrieked a bridesmaid. Dhaka smiled edgily.

"Jess," Sophie exclaimed, shoving her face forward for more kisses. The introductions halted the conversation. To fill the silence, Jess asked her foolish question about Dhaka's name.

"Oh, I was conceived there. Speaking of social Darwinism…"

"Those are Dhaka's parents," Tom said quietly, nodding at a couple in the far corner whom Jess had already crossed off her list of possibles: she in Laura Ashley, he in a cowboy hat, both balancing coffee cups on their elbows, not talking to anyone. Jess thought they looked frightened.

"What I'd like to do," Dhaka said, "is round up all the cunts and introduce them to Lilith."

"He's pissed," Sophie said.

"He's a raving Tory!" said someone else.

Jess felt the devil rising in her. "Sophie, remember when we marched in that Amnesty International protest in New York? We rode a Greyhound bus all night to get there." She pumped her fist in the air. "Free Mumia Abu-Jamal!"

After a second, everyone laughed.

"Banquo's ghost," Tom murmured, the corners of his eyes creasing.

The argument revived. It seemed to have to do with the rights of citizens in a democratic society, and Jess had plenty of opinions about that, but gradually she realized that what they were all doing actually was taking the piss out of Dhaka. It was like watching a pick-up basketball game: enthralling, even if you were fuzzy on the rules. Jess probably never would master the English art of the piss-take, but that didn't mean she could not appreciate it.

Soon, Sophie grew bored and started to ask her about their classmates from Bennington, and that was even better. But Jess could feel herself flagging. As the conversation moved on to gossip about people she did not know, she allowed herself to be led by Louise down a pink-wallpapered passage that turned two angles, without any doors on either side, and ended in a single bed that took up the whole width of the corridor, a window at its head and a chest-of-drawers at its foot. "We're really jamming people into the cracks," Louise apologized. "But you should be OK here. Far enough from the madding crowd to sleep."

In fact she could still hear them through the walls, but as

soon as Louise left her, she sank into unconsciousness. Someone touched her shoulder and said that everyone was going to the pub – did she want to come? Lucidly, she said, "Oh, I'd love to," and rose, but her limbs were bloated and heavy; they would not move. The person retreated from her down the corridor, towards a strange sullen yellow light, and Jess toppled back onto the bed, understanding that she had never woken up at all.

The weather that had been denied them for the wedding broke gloriously over the coast the next day, filling the lane with cars, and the cove – visible at an angle from the kitchen windows of the Garnett house – with sunbathers and snorkellers.

After a protracted brunch, the houseguests staggered down to the cove and claimed the rocks at the near end, below the low stone wall that separated the cove from the end of the lane. Jess spread her towel next to Tom Fairweather's and lay on her back, recklessly soaking up the sun. "I feel like a political prisoner released from jail," she said. "I feel like I'm about to split open." She sketched an incision down her stomach. "Inside, I'm really a butterfly."

"You should have come with us to the pub last night."

"Oh, I'm so mad at myself that I missed it. Was it a lot of fun?"

Tom shrugged. "Everyone got sloshed. Dhaka had a row with his uncle."

"That must have been entertaining." I'm starting to talk like them, Jess thought, smiling at herself.

"It was… predictable." Tom lay face up, sunglasses on his nose. In trunks, he was very white.

"Put some sunblock on," Jess said. "Do you want some of mine?"

"Thanks, but there's not much point if we're going in the water later…" He turned his head towards her. "Sorry. I've just got a bit of a hangover."

"That's all right."

"Jess!" Sophie screamed from further down the stony beach. "Tom, you wimp! Come on, I dare you!"

The water was so cold that Jess's muscles ran with little fiery cramps. They all swam out to the nearest of the sea-weed-bearded buoys. Tom dunked Jess, and she splashed him back, and their laughter seemed to fly up in arcs and fall back into the trillion sparkling wavelets that splintered in her eyes and filled her mouth with a taste like a memory she had lost, or maybe a loss she remembered only in her DNA: the collective human longing for home.

The horizon bristled with boats. From the woods on the opposite arm of the cove poked a grey stone gable, diamond-paned. "That's our neighbor," Sophie said. "She's put up electric fences to stop the day-trippers from trespassing on her property. I wish Mum would, too – I mean, look at them."

The beach was chock-a-block, and an icecream van had set up behind the stone wall.

"Would it be disgustingly traitorous of me to buy a cone?" Jess sank down on her towel and reached for her sunglasses case, where she had stashed a few pounds. Opening it, she drew back with a cry. Stickiness slid between her fingers. There was a briny smell like rotting seaweed. Black gunk dripped out of the case and splotted on her knee, separating into a gelatinous liquid filled with little transparent pearls like black frogspawn. It coated her money. Her sunglasses sat in the case with their legs folded like a crab's, swimming in the stuff.

"Oh God!" She emptied the case onto the rock. The gunk slid away into a crevice, leaving a tacky trail that instantly began to flake at the edges. "Look at this!" She was wiping her sunglasses with her towel, and everyone was staring at her. "Someone must have fucked with my shit while we were in the water. Oh *yuck.*" She laughed and shuddered.

"Ewww," Sophie said faintly.

"Imagine it was supposed to be a joke," said one of Dhaka's London friends. "I'd say you've got an admirer, Jess."

"Oh no! No way!"

"Oh yes way, and as chief suspects I'd propose..." He nodded in the direction of a group of teenage boys parked on the shale below their rocks.

"Little shits," Dhaka said. "It's your call, Jess. Do you want us to deal with them – or leave them to Lilith?" Everyone laughed.

"Oh – oh, I think leave them to Lilith," Jess said, still not understanding this bit of slang. But the men nodded approvingly.

"That's the smart choice. Don't react. Only encourages them."

"Too late for that," Jess muttered, still trying to get the gunk off the lenses of her sunglasses, where it was drying in a crackly coating.

"Here," Tom said. He took the sunglasses and trickled water from his Evian bottle over them.

"Thank you. What... what do you think it *is?*"

"Probably not anything you'd want to get in your mouth." Jess lowered her hand; she had been about to bite her nails, a habit supposedly conquered long ago. "Not actually toxic, I don't think they'd go that far. But why don't you go back in the water and have a splash around, just to be on the safe side?"

Jess did as she was told. Returning, she dried herself with the un-gunky bits of her towel. "Now I really need an icecream."

"I should have thought of that. My treat."

They sat and licked their soft-serve cones, the sun baking their faces, the wind raising goosepimples on their backs.

"The only thing is, I don't think it *was* a joke," Jess said.

"Why not?"

"It wasn't funny!"

"There's nothing more subjective than humor," Tom said. "Look, I really don't think you should dwell on it. *That's* giving them what they want. It was nasty, it's over, now let's enjoy the sunshine."

Jess wrinkled her nose disconsolately. She wanted to talk

about it, as if words could make it comprehensible. But she was getting into the habit of doing as Tom said and so she followed his gaze out to sea. "That's a millionaire's toy," she said presently.

A double-decked motor cruiser was powering a slow course towards them. There seemed to be a party going on aboard; the faint rhythm of rock music jangled across the waves, and groups of people stood on the upper and lower decks. To a man and woman they wore black, their silhouettes outlandish, tightly massed. All of them seemed to be facing ashore, staring at the people in the cove. Jess shivered as the yacht ploughed slowly past the rocks. "They look like they came straight out of the Bermuda Triangle."

"Oh, they'll be friends of Lilith's," Sophie said, overhearing. "She's got an anchorage on the far side of the point." Supine in her little white bikini, she squinted down at her stomach. "Shit, I think I'm burning." She waited. "Now I know chivalry is dead," she said.

"I have to go back in for my wrap, anyway," Jess said. "It's kind of chilly after you come out of the water. How about I get you something to cover up with?"

"Bless you, Jess! My caftan's on the hook in the hall. If you can't find it, Louise'll show you."

But when Jess reached the house, the front door was locked. "Shit!" Mincing over the gravel in her bare feet, she edged around the house. Now that she could not get in, she very much wanted to – perhaps to sprawl on her funny corridor bed and succumb to a dreamless sleep that would carry her away from gothically overloaded yachts and gunk in sunglasses cases. Knocking on windows raised only odd echoes – *clunk, clunk;* she spun and saw that at least one of the cars was gone. Louise must have taken Frieda, Sophie's married sister, and the little ones shopping.

Around the side of the house she found another door, laid her palms on green paint warmed by the sun, and turned the handle. The door swung open. She padded into a sitting-room she hadn't yet seen, with hassocks and large windows facing Louise's straggly vegetable garden. A segment of a school blackboard leaned against the wall by the fireplace, covered with sentences in colored chalk.

I love Lilith, she read; it was the largest sentence by far, right at the bottom of the board.

Lilith cares for my children.
Lilith showed me how to go to bed properly.
Lilith likes people to be comfortable with who they are.

And all over the board, erased ghosts hovered: *Lilith Lilith Lilith Lilith Lilith Lilith Lilith looks after her own*

A Lot of Things about Lilith (Only Some of Which are True), Jess thought. Her giggle sounded to her like a squeak. She blundered out of the room and forced her way through the house until she reached the front hall. She grabbed Sophie's caftan and turned the latch of the Yale to let herself out. Had she closed the other door? If she hadn't, too bad. She wasn't going back in there.

She hurried back down the lane, tossed the caftan to Sophie, then squatted on the rocks beside Tom, rolling up her towel. "I'm leaving," she said in a low voice. "Please don't tell anyone until after I've gone."

Tom sat up. "How? I mean, how are you going to go?" He did not ask *why,* she noted.

"I don't know. Hitchhike."

"I'll give you a ride," he said, standing up, and then of course all the others asked them where they were going. It must have shown on their faces.

"Just making a run into town," Tom said. "Anything you want us to pick up?"

"Oh, Je-ess," Sophie whined, her face scrunched up like a selfish little girl's, just the way she had looked ten years ago when she particularly wanted Jess to carry out some unpleasant duty for her. "We've only *got* today and tomorrow!"

"Just making a run into town!" Jess echoed Tom. "Be right back!"

"You weren't scared by that joke we played on you?" Dhaka smiled, stretched out as long as a lion on his towel. "It was only – you could consider it an initiation."

"Jess knows that," Tom said firmly. "Stop giving her a hard time."

He vaulted over the stone wall: Jess followed him. They knew, they all knew that she was running away, she could feel it in their mocking gazes, but she no longer cared, as long as they did not stop her from leaving.

She had decided to abandon her belongings, but she reluctantly agreed to go in for them when Tom offered to accompany her. They walked down the twisting corridor to the jammed-in bed; the pink walls seemed to pulse and strain to close on them like a throat. Jess threw her things into her suitcase, and did not exhale until she had thrown the suitcase into the trunk *(boot)* of Tom's car, a little beige Fiat.

Somewhat to her surprise, it started easily.

She slumped into the passenger seat while the trees ticked past faster and faster, feeling vastly relieved and – now – more than a little foolish. "Sorry. I mean, thank you. I just – "

"No need to explain. I felt the same way the first time I came here. I understand."

But she wanted him to do more than understand, or say he understood, which did not necessarily amount to the same thing. If only he was not so very English!

"The stuff in my sunglasses case – "

"Spawn. Yes."

She fought for breath. "Spawn of *what?*"

"Getting into deep waters there, I'm afraid. Truly, Jess, you'd better leave well enough alone."

"But it's *not* well enough! Sophie – Dhaka – Louise – "

"They're all hers already. Nothing to be done about that. Jess, please stop asking questions or I'll have to kill you."

Trees and voluptuous English hedgerows flashed past; lanes wriggled away untaken; the silence in the car hardened.

Finally Jess said in an artificial voice, "Tom, you don't have to take me all the way to Plymouth. This is far enough, really. I can walk the rest of the way. Thanks."

"Plymouth? Don't be silly, I'm taking you back to London."

"Oh, but – it's *miles* – "

"You wouldn't be safe anywhere closer to her. I think she almost got you last night, as it is."

Jess started to cry. Tom flashed a glance at her, then returned his gaze to the road.

"Please," she sobbed, fumbling with the door, although the child safety locks were down. "Stop. Please. Why won't you stop?"

"I don't know about you," Tom said, "but to me that sounds like a question."

She risked a look at him; his lips had pulled back, exposing his teeth in a grimace. She hunched her head down and covered her face with her hands.

Through her fingers she saw that black liquid, slimy, clotted with tiny globules, had started to ooze around the edges of the glove compartment and drip to the rubber-matted floor.

WALKING ALL THE WAY

On her first day in Tokyo, Devin woke disoriented but filled with a sense of optimism. Sunbeams streaked across her sleeping-bag from the gap between the curtains of Margrethe and Tatsuya's living-room. A heart-beat later she remembered her breakup with Chaz: the grief, the shouting, the dreary U-Haul trek back to her mother's house in New Jersey. She thought about all that for a few seconds, and then, slowly but undiminished, her optimism returned.

She got up and stepped between the curtains, through the open window onto the balcony, where a few spider plants and sanseverias looked as if they needed watering. Stretching her arms high, she squinched her face up and wriggled from head to toe in the sunlight like a child under a fire hydrant. She opened her eyes; across thirty feet of air she met the gaze of a woman who was hanging out her futons on

15

the balcony of a neighboring building. The woman stared at her.

Four storeys below, a tailless cat scuttered across the path of a postman on a motorized tricycle, balked at nothing, and dived behind a stack of recycling bins.

Devin plunged back into the apartment, giggling. "I think I just traumatized your neighbor."

Margrethe stood in the kitchen, which was separated from the living-room by an accordion screen of flower-printed vinyl. She shook coffee into the french press. "Do them good," she said. "Anyway, no one talks to their neighbors in Tokyo. I've never even seen the people next door."

"Just like New York."

"Only more so."

The rich scent of coffee filled the apartment. The two girls sat at the kitchen table and resumed last night's conversation where they had left off.

"I can't believe we haven't seen each other since your wedding," Devin said, smiling at the memory. Margrethe and Tatsuya had been married in Hawaii, with leis for everyone. "How is Tatsuya, anyway? I can't believe I missed him…" She had passed out on her air mattress before Margrethe's husband returned from work last night, and he had already been gone when she awoke this morning.

"Oh, that's totally normal. He never gets home before midnight. Sometimes it's like two or three a.m.; the company pays his taxi fare… But he's taking Saturday off so we can all do something."

"Doesn't he always get Saturday off?"

"Oh no. *Oh* no." Margrethe rose. Tallish and hippy, she had a delicate face framed by the fine blond hair of her Danish ancestors. "Dev, it's almost noon! Why are we still slopping around in here? I want to show you everything. I promised Tatsuya we'd leave Akihabara until Saturday, but we could go to Shinjuku Gyoen – that's a really gorgeous park – or Yasukuni Shrine, or just wander around Shibuya. Or do the museums. There are billions of museums I've never even been to." She cocked her head. "Or we could always…"

"Go shopping," Devin said.

"Go shopping," Margrethe finished almost simultaneously, and both of them burst into laughter.

"You are kidding. You have got to be kidding me." Devin struggled out of the skirt and peeked around the curtain of the changing cubicle. "Mar, can you see if they've got a bigger size?"

Margrethe spoke to the sales clerk. Her Japanese was fluent, but even Devin could hear that it did not sound like Japanese as the Japanese themselves spoke it. She sounded as if she were speaking English, only with nonsense in place of words. At any rate the sales clerk understood. A moment later Margrethe came back to the changing cubicle, shaking her head. "You've got the M, right? That's the largest size."

"There is no way that was an M! That was like an XS."

"I told you, I don't even try to buy clothes anywhere except The Gap."

"Yes, but…" Devin was smaller than her friend; she wore an 8, sometimes a 6. "Oh well. I guess maybe I could fit into a sweater or something."

"Or a t-shirt," Margrethe said. "Hey!"

The sun poured down on Takeshita Street. Everyone looked to Devin like Gwen Stefani's Harajuku Girls, including the boys. The cramped little shops, spilling lace and tartan and sneakers and leather goods onto the sidewalk, reminded her of a bazaar in the Arab world, but without the haggling. She had already bought a Hello Kitty wallet and a pair of skull-and-crossbones earrings. Now a cornucopia of vintage and novelty t-shirts beckoned.

Rape Me.

"Kurt Cobain could get away with it," Margrethe said.

Miso Horny.

"That's actually kind of funny."

"Yeah, it has to be stupid funny, not funny funny."

変な外人.

"This means *Weird Foreigner.*"

"Ouch. I'm not sure I can carry off such profundity."

Zoom Hero Drive Fast.

"Ditto."

Fuckin' 西洋.

"Oh Dev, you have to get this one."

"What's it mean?"

"Fuckin' Occident."

"Are you sure that's not too profound for me?"

"No, you can get away with it because you're Jewish. So it's not even ironic self-hate, it's like a political protest."

"I think it's illegal to wear obscenities on t-shirts in America."

"Is it? Well, you can always put a patch over the *u* or something. Look, they've got patches at the register. A star, or…"

Devin emerged from the shop with *Fuckin'* 西洋 stretched across her bosom, a patch over the *u* of a smiley face with a bullet hole in its forehead. Margrethe had bought the same patch to put on her work satchel.

Laughing, arms brushing, they wandered down Takeshita Street to Meiji Avenue, bought sandwiches to go at Aux Bacchanales, detoured into the surrealist shopping mall of LaForet, and finally circled up to Jingu Bridge, a graceful stone arch where a handful of punks and goths sat around not listening to the buskers. "The real cosplayers aren't here. They come out on weekends," Margrethe said. "Gothic lolitas, French maids, you name it."

"Oh my God, that guy totally looks like Sweeney Todd. Do you think they'd mind if I took pictures?"

"I think it would make their day."

They ate their sandwiches in Yoyogi Park. It was a late lunch: the sunlight had already started to slant amber between the trees. "And now I have to go," Margrethe said, draining her Diet Pepsi. "Dev – this is awful of me, but can I leave you to get home by yourself? I mean can you find the way? If not —"

"I'm sure I can find the way, but—" Devin was confused. "Mar, do you have to work this evening? You should've said!"

Margrethe was an English teacher who worked odd hours, roving among her clients' corporate offices. Today she wore capri jeans and a flowered blouse. "Not in this. No, I took the day off, but - oh, Dev, can I tell you a secret? I mean you've got to guard it with your *life.*"

"I can't believe you didn't tell me already," Devin howled. "Of course you can."

"I just didn't want to - I mean, after you and Chaz, and the last time you saw me and Tatsuya we were so happy, and I didn't want to spoil your illusion…"

"When it comes to men, I have no illusions anymore," Devin said grimly.

Margrethe laughed weakly. "No, I guess you wouldn't. But anyway - I'm having an affair." She wrung her hands in her lap.

"I knew it," Devin said, after a barely perceptible pause. She was completely astonished. "But Mar, what's wrong with you and Tatsuya? I mean, he seemed so nice—"

"See? That's exactly why - I mean, it's like impossible to explain. And I know objectively it is indefensible."

"No, oh my God, I totally support you. But couldn't you—"

"I *will* try to explain later. I promise. But right now I'm supposed to be meeting him in Shibuya like fifteen minutes ago. So—"

"Shit! Go on, then. I can find my way home, I'll just wander and enjoy myself a bit first… Be careful, 'kay?"

Margrethe leaned down and hugged her tightly. "You're a total star, Dev. Listen, if you get stuck anywhere, call me… and if Tatsuya comes home early, although he won't, tell him I have a private student. That's my alibi."

"You got it… Mar! Just one thing, OK, what's his name?"

Already turning to rush off, Margrethe paused and smiled. It was not her usual smile; it made her look sappy.

"Philip," she said. "His name's Philip."

Philip, who preferred to be known as Phil, leaned back against the scalloped, seashell-pink headboard, flipping through the faux-leather-bound album that described the offerings of the Dolphin Hotel's entertainment center. Karaoke, porn with mosaics over the interesting bits, a selection of movies (mostly Hollywood fare)... He lingered over the video games. Pathetic, really, that anyone who had managed to steal a few hours with his lover should then waste them on Sonic the Hedgehog. Clearly, though, there was a demand... He switched on NHK and half-heartedly tried to guess what the politicians were expostulating about.

The sluicing of the shower ceased. Margrethe padded out of the bathroom, a towel knotted around her generous hips. She was ashamed of her body, Phil knew. They had had long conversations about the insanity of the media and its stereotypes of physical beauty – this was before they became lovers – but he had not yet been able to convince her that she was beautiful. Her smile had an edge of insecurity as she exposed herself to him now, outwardly casual. "So, any resolution on the beef ban?"

"Is that what they're talking about?" As he spoke, the TV switched to a scene of brawling protesters in Korea.

"It's a symbolic issue, of course," Margrethe said, settling beside him. "They're banning American beef imports because they can't ban American cultural imports."

"Unfortunately." Phil curved an arm around her back and squeezed a breast. "So why haven't I seen you in class this week?"

Phil was Margrethe's yoga instructor.

"I've got a friend from America staying. I've been busy cleaning up, getting the apartment ready for her..." She jumped up. "Oh my God, I forgot! I've got to show you what I found in the bathroom."

She vanished into the lighted rectangle of the bathroom door and re-emerged a moment later, pulling a large rectangular mat that would have done as a yoga mat if it were a little longer.

"It's a Love Mat," she said, giggling. "Look."

The dimpled surface bore the legend LOVE MAT and depicted a chubby cartoon couple in a variety of coital poses. "Kama Sutra for Dummies," Phil said, shaking his head. "Listen, I know the Japanese really like following instructions. But this is just... I mean, this is a love hotel, right? If you've got this far, you presumably *know* how to make *love*, right? Or is the problem a lack of imagination?" He flicked the cartoon man's genital area with a fingernail. "Actually, I feel sorry for anyone who finds this stimulating."

Margrethe went off in gales of laughter that sounded slightly forced. "But we've got to try it out," she said. "Since it's here."

"I... have no objection to that." Phil leered. "But first..." He tugged on the knot of her towel. It fell. "Guruji says no pain, no progress."

"Do we have to?"

"Yes, Margrethe, because I care about your practise."

Wrinkling her nose resignedly, Margrethe placed her feet together and steepled her hands in front of her chest. "Ommm," she intoned.

"Ommm," Phil joined in, and the doors of his mind gently irised shut, turning his head into an echo chamber empty of carnal desire. He was no longer even tempted to eye Margrethe's body. "Om vande gurunam charanaravinde..."

The room smelt of stale cigarette smoke. In one wall, a vending machine dispensed dildoes and other sex toys from clear perspex drawers. In the other wall, heavy wooden shutters kept out any chink of light from the world beyond. The ceiling over the bed bore clusters of LEDs in the shapes of constellations, which blinked down unheeded upon Phil and Margrethe as they stretched, inhaled, and exhaled their way through a series of sun salutations.

Shivering with contentment, Devin settled onto a stool facing the great glass wall of the hotel bar and raised her Kir Royale to the view that rolled from horizon to horizon. Spiky neon fish swam in the gathering twilight, amid dark spires and towers whose great height appeared less from this even greater height. She seemed to be floating on a level with the remnant of the sunset that stained the western sky like the echoes of a shout, orange now fading to lemon and an eerie green. Classical music tinkled through the bar. She felt pleased with herself for successfully finding this place. Also, she felt very glamorous. In her joke t-shirt and canvas wraparound skirt, she knew that she probably looked like a typical tourist. But glamor was a state of mind, she thought. It was how she felt about her future: a sense of shapeless anticipation.

"Cheers." The voice came from her left. She tore her gaze from the view and faced a youngish Indian man, tieless, with a plump melancholy countenance.

"Oh." She clinked her drink against his beer. "Cheers."

"This is the place where *Lost in Translation* was filmed, you know."

"I know," Devin said, grinning. "That's why I'm here."

"It is very beautiful."

"Yes," although *beautiful* was not the word she would have chosen; *beautiful* was landscapes and animals, not post-industrial metropolises. But then again, what if she was wrong about that and the Indian man right?

"Where are you from?"

"New York," Devin said. "America. What about you?"

"I am from Delhi. But I live here now. I have my own company."

"Wow. Excellent."

"Yes, I have my own company, I have people working for me, but I have no friends."

"Oh dear," Devin said, shifting away a little. "Why not?"

"I have no time. Always working, always busy."

"You're not working now," she pointed out.

"Recently I have a little time. So I am looking for a girl."

"Oh. Well…"

"I am looking for a girl with a good pure heart."

"Oh," Devin said. "Well, that's a very commendable ambition. Quite a challenge, though." She thought of Margrethe and then of herself. "I mean, you've set the bar kind of high."

The Indian man's smile sagged. Lifting his chin, perceptibly bracing himself, he said hopelessly, "You are very beautiful."

For a moment Devin felt poisonously resentful. How dare he interrupt her private happy hour, and then compound the offense by hitting on her? With a mental effort, she recognized the absurdity of her own complaint, and summoned a smile. "Thank you," she said. "That's really nice to hear. I'm afraid I have to go now —" she slipped off her stool, leaving an inch of Kir Royale in the bottom of her glass — "but I really do hope you find what you're looking for."

The Indian man's parting smile held a valedictory warmth that both reassured and humbled her. At least he knew what he was looking for, she reflected.

She took the long way back to the elevators, drinking in the view once more from close up. The sunset had faded to a wash of gradually dulling blue: the neon kanji glowed and flashed.

Swinging his briefcase, relishing the warm evening into which he had escaped at the almost unheard-of hour of seven thirty, Tatsuya strolled homeward along the arcade of little shops near the station. The street seemed unfamiliar, it had been so long since he got home before everything closed. The tofu-maker and the senbei-baker were serving customers beneath the arc lights clipped to their awnings, the butcher in his wellingtons slapped pork chops onto the scale, the greengrocer totaled purchases on her abacus, the take-away sushi shop was doing a brisk trade. Because he could, he bought a box of inari-zushi and maki-zushi, but he stopped off anyway at the Seven-Eleven at the end of the arcade for beer and cigarettes. The fluorescent-lit shelves were more familiar to him than the contents of his own refrigerator. At the check-out, he reached into the hot drinks case and drew out a can of café au lait; considered; added another.

He sipped the first can as he rounded the corner by the dry-cleaner's. A man leaned against the scabrous tiled wall, one geta sandal kicked back against the curb, cleaning his fingernails with a curved knife twenty centimeters long. He wore his glossy black hair in a folded-over knot at the back of his skull. A rough sash fastened his faded indigo kimono. The straps of his sandals were frayed. Tatsuya stopped in front of him. "Nice evening, isn't it?"

The man lifted his gaze. "I walked all the way," he said.

"I know," Tatsuya said. "Want a coffee?"

The man appeared to think about that for a moment, then nodded. Tatsuya reached into his Seven-Eleven bag and took out the second can of café au lait. The man thrust his knife into the scabbard almost concealed by the folds of his sash before accepting the coffee the polite way, with both hands. The thumb that popped the tab was broad, callused, the nail gnarled but trimmed and clean.

"I got off work early," Tatsuya said. "Thought you might not be here yet."

"I have nowhere else to be. Yet."

Tatsuya smiled, hunched one shoulder in a half-shrug. "Smoke?"

"Thank you, I would be grateful."

They smoked their cigarettes in silence, watching homeward-bound salarymen and career women hurry past. A tailless tabby cat minced out of the privet hedge on the other side of the roadway and arched its back, hissing. Tatsuya sighed, threw down his cigarette, and trod on it. "Well, I'd better be getting back. I get to eat supper at home for once; what a treat. My wife might even be there, with her friend."

"Have you told them yet?"

"Them?"

"Your superiors."

Tatsuya winced.

In a moment of exhausted frustration last week, he had resolved to tell his boss point blank that the project was going to be a failure, they simply did not have enough bodies and were not efficiently using the ones they had, they were going to miss their deadline. But that would mean going behind the back of his team leader, who was stopping all complaints at the source and pretending that everything was fine. To make matters worse, Tatsuya was indebted to the team leader through long acquaintance. He was not yet prepared to take the momentous step of ratting him out for incompetence. "I was kind of pissed off with life that day," he said. "I need more time to decide what I'm going to do."

"Think about it, then." The other man's black eyes were hard. He knew Tatsuya was stalling.

"I will." Tatsuya raised a hand and walked away without looking back.

Finding the front door of the apartment unlocked, he had time to prepare himself to meet Margrethe's friend Devin. She was curled up on the sofa, reading a paperback.

"Hi," she said, sitting up. She looked nervous. Maybe she was shy of him. They had only met once before, in Hawaii.

"Hi, Devin. Where's Margrethe?"

"Oh, she – she had a private student. She didn't think you'd get home so early – hee hee! – but she should be back soon. Yep." Devin splayed her book on the arm of the sofa and followed him into the kitchen. "Is that your dinner?"

"Yes. Have you eaten?"

"Oh, I had sushi, too – some of those hand rolls from the little shop up there. Umm! Those were good."

Tatsuya halted his chopsticks. "Do you like sushi?"

"I love it! I eat sushi for lunch almost every day at home. Uh, from the Korean deli. You'd probably think it wasn't the real thing."

"Well, if you'd like a drink or anything... coffee, tea... beer... anything you like. Feel free." He waved a hand vaguely.

"Oooh, I'd love a beer."

Not without a pang, Tatsuya handed her one of the cans of Asahi he had bought for himself. She sat across the kitchen table from him and sipped it, bright-eyed. To break the silence he asked her about her plans. She said she had bought a two-week rail pass and intended to travel all over the country, staying in youth hostels.

"I was thinking of leaving on Sunday. But actually now I think I might go sooner than that. Like maybe tomorrow, even."

"What? Why? You can stay here as long as you like."

Devin gazed abstractedly at the corner of the ceiling. "Well, I mean, even though you guys are being so fantastic about putting me up, and I can't imagine, if I had to stay in a hotel it would be ridiculous – but I'm supposed to be on a budget, and I spent like a hundred dollars today, just on food and getting around, and a bit of shopping…"

"Yes, the prices are very high in Tokyo," Tatsuya agreed. Suddenly he felt expansive, kindlier towards her. He put his used chopsticks into the empty sushi box and stuffed it into the trash. "Now I'm going to play my guitar. I hope I don't disturb you. Tell me if it's too noisy."

While he played Eric Clapton and the Beatles, she sat with her nose in her book, occasionally looking around at an infelicitous chord. But when he launched into "Paranoid," her book went down, her head came up, and she began to sing along under her breath.

"You know Black Sabbath, Devin? No, go on, please! You have a nice voice."

In truth it was reedy, but she could carry a tune. Loosening up, she got to her feet and swayed as she sang. Tatsuya turned up the volume and rocked out. Suddenly the doorbell chimed.

"Shit, it's the neighbors!"

"Oh no," Devin giggled.

An idea came to him. "Can you get it? Just say I'm not

here, OK?"

She hurried to the door. Skulking in the kitchen, Tatsuya heard a woman apologizing profusely. He grinned to himself. The door closed; Devin skipped back into the room. "I think it's OK. Of course, I couldn't understand what she was saying—"

"She apologized to *you!*" Tatsuya laughed. "She came to ask us to turn it down – and *she* apologized to *you!* She must have been terrified when she saw you were a foreigner, and…" He gurgled, getting control of his mirth. "That was the first time they've ever come over here, and I think it'll be the last time, too."

Devin looked confused, then cautiously amused; then she grinned. "So, do you know any more Black Sabbath?"

They did "Crazy Train" and "Mr. Crowley," and had just moved on to Deep Purple when the doorbell rang again.

"Damn," Devin said. "Well, I know how to handle her now. Just look like a scary foreigner. I should've bought that other t-shirt."

Crouched in the corner of the living-room with his amp buzzing quietly beside him, Tatsuya frowned. Instead of the woman's voice, he heard the brief burr of a man's voice, followed by Devin's high-pitched English. The amp crackled. A faint whine of feedback emerged from its speaker and grew louder until Tatsuya wrenched the dial, turning it all the way down. His shoulders and the top of his scalp cramped with gooseflesh. He stood up.

Devin came back into the room. "It wasn't the neighbor," she said. "Not the same one, anyway."

Pretending insouciance, Tatsuya sat down on the arm of the sofa and played a couple of chords that sounded tinny on the unplugged strings. "Was it a man?"

"Yeah. Oh, I guess you know him? He must have thought I was Margrethe, because he asked me, 'Where is your husband?' And I was like, uh, I'm not married – it didn't occur to me at that point that he thought I was Margrethe – and he just said, 'There is much further to go.' I mean, what does *that* mean? It was *weird*… he looked so *tired*… and he was also dressed weird." She blushed. "I mean, not weird, but… he was wearing a kimono."

"I know him." He urgently wanted to ask her: *Did he have the knife?* But if he *had,* surely she'd be alarmed. "It probably wasn't important. You can forget it."

"But it was weird," Devin said. Hugging herself, she added in a whisper that sounded almost happy: "There's so much I still don't understand about this country."

The doorbell rang for a third time. Tatsuya let out a choked-off yell.But it was only Margrethe, flushed and happy, who had given her keys to Devin earlier and now needed to be let in.

The Japanese rail system covers the archipelago like a spidery exoskeleton. Into this metal map of journeys past and present Devin set out, feeling like a mouse scurrying through the scaffolding of an alien architectural project. Every station had multiple levels and platforms; every youth hostel seemed to be a long walk away at the top of a hill. The railroads both made available and obscured the baroque marvels of the countryside. Craggy mountains and lush rice paddies, suburban sprawl, hamlets and highrise provincial capitals… she saw them all from train windows, and wondered about the lives of the people who lived there, people who did not travel. Her intense curiosity played out in comic encounters balked by the language barrier. There were also moments of tear-jerking kindness from strangers; there was the elderly man who followed her all through the town until, badly frightened, she screamed at him that she would call the police – that was enough to send him packing; and there were the conversations in youth-hostel kitchens and lounges with Japanese backpackers who more or less spoke English. Hippie-scarved, chain-smoking, they talked mostly about the other places they had been. Prague, Marrakesh, Ulan Bator, Rio de Janeiro… after a while these remote destinations all started to sound the same to Devin. But when she asked them about their own lives, they had nothing to say, or would not say it. They advised her to visit this mountain, that festival, the other onsen.

So she went to the hot springs and boiled herself lobster-pink. She hiked up a mountain and ate black "onsen tamago." She hugged an eight-hundred-year-old tree, almost got bitten by a monkey, took pictures of schoolchildren in their adorable little yellow beanies, and got mixed up quite by accident in a local festival, among a crowd of half-naked men jigging through the streets with a gold-encrusted shrine on their shoulders. That night she drank at an izakaya with the bon vivant seniors who had adopted her into their midst, and woke flat on her back on a grassy roadside. Terror gripped her. She had no idea where she was in the universe. But her head was resting on her backpack, and in the mesh pocket her hand encountered a packet of manju dumplings, sweet bean paste snugged into soft pastry shells, wrapped in a cotton handkerchief. She unwrapped them and ate one, sitting there on the verge, somewhere so remote that not a single car was passing. Above her the stars cavorted with the clouds. The message had grown clearer now, she could almost decipher it – but then the clouds thickened, and the intricate pattern of lights was lost.

At last she turned back towards Tokyo. She did not want to go. She felt like Pandora, if that demigoddess, hand already on the latch, had been called away to catch a train, leaving her box unopened. All she'd done was admire the patterns on the outside. But her rail pass was about to expire; as the Japanese said, *sho ga nai* – there was no help for it.

A shinkansen roared past, pushing a storm front of wind. Rain rattled on the skylights of the station. There was a cloying smell of broth from the soba and udon stand. She bought a can of sweet coffee from a vending machine and sipped it. Really, this stuff was weirdly delicious; or maybe it was just that the taste always teased her with some elusive memory of something else she had eaten or drunk, perhaps in a dream… Mentally, now, she was half back in Tokyo already.

Checking her email at last night's youth hostel, she had found a message from Margrethe. Tatsuya had accepted an invitation to fill in at the next gig of a band led by some guy he knew; the show was on the day of Devin's scheduled return. If she were not too tired, would she like to go?

Too tired? She was tingling with energy, on edge with anticipation. The best part of her trip now lay behind her, but her neurochemistry did not seem to have gotten the message – or maybe her body knew something she did not. All the way back to Tokyo she struggled to figure out what it was telling her.

Five floors up from an alleyway in Sangenjaya, above a ya-kiniku restaurant and a vintage clothes retailer and a graphic design company and a recording studio, the rock café Heaven's Gate consisted of a room with a stage at one end and another room with sofas, separated by a wall that was mostly arches. In front of the stage milled a handful of people who knew the performers personally.

Beer in hand, Devin stood with Margrethe and Phil, jiggling from foot to foot to the beat of Aerosmith as interpreted by Kubikirizoku featuring Tatsuya on guitar. Margrethe had explained to her that Tatsuya knew Phil as her yoga instructor and one of her friends. All the same, Devin felt terribly tense, as if the truth about Margrethe and Phil were out but everyone was being too polite to notice it.

What made it all the more difficult was that she had more or less come down on Tatsuya's side, and meeting Phil had not changed her mind. He was an inch shorter than Margrethe, with a gentle smile and a trick of looking you in the eye for too long without blinking. His cargo shorts exposed hairy shins. Mildly he bopped to "Mama Kin," his smile unchanging, and laughter welled up in Devin's throat like hiccups.

"It is still much further."

She turned. A few feet away stood Margrethe and Tatsu-ya's neighbor, the man in the scruffy blue kimono. She started to go towards him, but he gave a curt shake of his head. "What do you mean? What do you *mean?*" she said fretfully, only then realizing, in the back of her mind, how odd it was that she could understand him at all – that a man so traditionally Japanese-looking should speak flawless English. But then again, why should he not?

"Not that way. This way." He turned and moved off towards the back of the room.

Gripped by urgent curiosity, exulting in it, Devin started to follow, but within a couple of paces she lost sight of him and stopped, disconsolate.

All the lights went off. Simultaneously the guitar and bass fell silent, leaving only the drummer and the vocalist, unamplified, to accompany each other for an instant before they were drowned out by cries of humorous alarm. A tinge of streetlight seeped through from the other room, which had windows.

The black shape that was Tatsuya lifted its guitar over its head, set it on the floor, and plunged down off the stage. Someone let out a raw shout.

In front of Devin a scuffle broke out. She was thrown staggering back as if from a moshpit. Margrethe shrieked. Devin fought to reach her side, but an angular square-winged shape loomed up in front of her; a hand seized her by the shoulder and spun her around.

She reached up. Inspired with a sudden certainty, she delicately unpicked the hard, warm fingers from her shoulder and laced her own fingers through them.

Now light from the hall illuminated the exit, and there were people clustered around it. Devin was not leading, but neither was she being led. She knew the way.

Someone located the breaker switch. The lights came back on and revealed Phil sitting on the floor in front of the stage. Gingerly, he touched his left eye. Blood trickled from his nose and down to his lips.

31

"**I** can't fucking believe you!" Margrethe wanted to scream at Tatsuya, but she restrained herself to a whisper.

No one else, except for maybe Phil himself, seemed to be aware that it was Tatsuya who had hit him. She had dragged Tatsuya into the other room and backed him up against one of the sofas by the windows.

A dopey grin of self-satisfaction spread across his face. "What, you think I'm going to let him fuck my wife and not do anything about it?"

"You *knew?*"

"I know *you.* I'm not stupid."

"But you are a coward," she hissed. "Or why'd you wait until the lights conveniently happened to go off?"

"It seemed like a good opportunity." Tatsuya nursed his knuckles. There was a small cut on one of them. He sucked it. "Why did you do it, anyway?" he said indistinctly.

"Why?" She raised her shoulders, let them fall. Her protean emotions hurled her in the other direction now. "Why *not,* when I never see you? Why not, when we never get to spend time together or even fucking *talk?* I thought I was marrying you, but little did I know you were already married to that goddamn company!"

Tatsuya's eyes went soft with the look of defensive incomprehension she knew so well. "I'm on a deadline. Our project—"

"You're always on a deadline! There's always some project!" Tears oozed down the sides of her nose. "There's not always going to be me."

Tatsuya's adam's apple hitched visibly. He said in a weak voice, "Sorry. Margrethe – I'm sorry."

"Dumbass. It's me who should be – *I'm* sorry."

Crying, she went into his arms.

Tatsuya sat on the sofa with Margrethe across his lap. When she seemed to have stopped crying, he shifted her head to his shoulder so he could light a cigarette.

She sat up. Then she rose on her knees. "Tatsuya! Oh my

God. Look."

He followed her pointing finger down through the window to the street. "Shit, that's—"

"*Yes,* it's Devin! Where's she going?"

"Oh, shit," Tatsuya mumbled. "Better go after her."

But he did not move. His consternation gave way to a feeling of guilty relief so powerful it made him lightheaded. Everything was clear now. It was not him, after all. He was safe.

Side by side at the window, they watched Devin walk away from the building and vanish amidst the fun-seekers: a calm, stolid little figure, apparently alone.

THE KINGDOM OF DARKNESS

"I feel like I can tell you anything," Haly said. She squinted intensely at Julia from behind a cloud of cigarette smoke that looked bluish in the afternoon sunlight.

Julia laughed at her, not believing it. "OK. So tell me why you got kicked out of prep school."

"Because I murdered my roommate." Haly grinned. She was the only full-tuition-paying, ex-Choate person Julia had ever met with crooked teeth. "You don't believe me, do you?"

The two girls were sitting on the broad steps that swept down from the administrative building in the center of campus. Other students sat scattered across the stone expanse, including Colton, who was lounging against the pedestal of the Alma Mater statue with Chloe Ryder sprawled across his legs. When he saw Julia and Haly crossing the steps, he had nudged Chloe and they had both waved, and for a moment

Julia had believed she could be friends with him and Chloe both. For a moment.

She tried not to let Haly see that her attention was wandering. "We-e-ell," she said. "If they caught you, why are you here? Why aren't you in some kind of juvenile offenders' lockdown?"

"Hey, I am. You are, we are. He, she, it is. Otherwise known as the Ivy League. No, they could never prove it, obviously. But they knew it was me. They threw me out a month later for violating the honor code, which was total bullshit."

Julia wrinkled her nose, disbelieving but still intrigued. She had admired Haly since they first met, during orientation, when a glance at Haly's notebook cover had revealed that her name was not *Halley* but *Haldita*. Whatever kind of name that was. Arabic? Haldita Fadow, black-wearing, cigarette-smoking, slightly overweight – but not snobbish, not in anyone's clique. Cool without being cruel. Or, so Julia had thought. "So how'd you do it?"

"How'd I kill her, you mean? I used my magic powers."

"Oh, *Haly*."

"Knew you wouldn't believe me." Haly lay back on her elbows and blew smoke up at the milky blue Manhattan sky.

"Well, I'm sure glad I'm not your roommate now," Julia said with a giggle.

"Meiying? I wouldn't do anything to hurt her. She doesn't bug me. We live, like, completely separate lives. That's the difference between college and boarding school."

"So, what, did your old roommate bug you?"

Haly rolled over on one elbow. "She was going to squeal on me. She *threatened* to squeal on me. So I had to make sure she wouldn't."

"Squeal on you about…"

"About my magic powers."

"That sounds all wrong," Julia said. "Like, it's a circular argument." She fell silent, distracted again by the sight of Chloe Ryder getting up to sit in Colton's lap.

Of course Chloe with her rock star dad, her angel tattoo in the small of her back and her studded belts that rode low on her slim hips. *Of course* not Julia, who had spent *(wasted,* she thought) all her high school years studying to get into this place, where she was still too shy and awkward to be cool. For here, everyone else (even Chloe Ryder) was *also* whip-smart, so that Julia had nothing left to distinguish her at all.

Julia and Chloe and Colton were in the same Contemporary Civilizations module. They had formed a study group, and Julia had jumped joyfully to the conclusion that this was fate's way of throwing her and Colton together. But week by week she had watched things going otherwise. Now, with hindsight, it had come to feel almost inevitable.

Almost inevitable, but not quite. After all, Chloe might dump Colton, or he might dump her...

"Well, if you've really got magic powers," she said, "can you do something about Chloe Ryder? Like, give her total *craters* all over her face?"

"Little Miss Rockstar? You know, Colton's going to see through her eventually. You just have to be there when he does."

"But when's *eventually* going to be?" Julia said hopelessly.

Haly's dark eyes softened. "I know," she said. She put her cigarette out on the step, frowning. "Acne? That might be tricky. How about something less... visible?"

"Hemorrhoids? Diarrhoea?"

"Not that kind of invisible," Haly said. "Like, metaphysical invisible. Hey, I could probably make her break up with him."

Julia hesitated. It seemed wrong. Then she remembered what her father always said. *Accepting failure is not in the Breckinridge playbook.* "Sure," she said. "Go for it."

"'Go for it!'" Haly snorted. "Dude, it's not that easy. I can't just wave my magic wand and utter some pig Latin. I need..." She trailed off thoughtfully.

Julia braced herself: a rat foetus, grave dust, a chalice full of virgin's blood... "Whatever you need, I'll try and get it for you."

"Two, three, get those knees up!"

Twenty-five teenagers in baggy t-shirts and sweatpants lumbered on and off their steps to a soundtrack of outdated pop and hip-hop. Julia had decided to get her gym requirement out of the way in freshman year, and step aerobics had sounded as if it would burn plenty of calories while requiring minimal physical coordination. Chloe had confided to her that she'd picked the class for a different reason: it met in the evening, and Chloe's policy was never to get out of bed before noon. Today, Chloe looked as if she were still groggy, her slender limbs moving sluggishly.

Now, Julia told herself, and stopped moving. She stood for a moment clutching her lower abdomen. Then she walked heavily to the front of the room. "Ms. Rodriguez, I feel kind of sick. It's that time of the month. Can I go sit down?"

"You girls, always the same excuse," Ms Rodriguez said loudly enough for the rest of the class to hear. "Women were menstruating for thousands of years before it occurred to them to get sick. They did not stop hunting and gathering because they had cramps!"

"Yes, Ms. Rodriguez, but I'm not a hunter-gatherer," Julia said. Giggles from the front row. Julia felt a twinge of panic. "I feel really terrible," she pleaded. "I have ibuprofen in my bag, can I go and take one?"

"Yes, yes, all right." Ms. Rodriguez dismissed her with a flick of long burgundy nails. "Come on, ladies! And one, two, pick it up..."

Julia crossed the running track, trotted along the balcony above the squash and volleyball courts, crossed the opposite loop of the track, and ducked into the locker room.

Voices and splashing echoed from the far end of the room, but it was not a peak hour and only a few compulsive exercisers were changing. Third aisle on the left. Empty, thank God. Only Julia's reflection in the mirror at the end of the aisle watched her open her own locker. She had taken care to put herself on the outside of Chloe so that the door of her own locker would partially hide Chloe's when it was opened. The lockers had locks, of course, but who ever bothered with them? Only students and faculty could use the gym, and you had to swipe your ID card to get in. Who was going to steal from you?

Heart pounding, Julia confronted the untidy pile of Chloe's clothes on the locker floor. Some faint expensive fragrance wafted from them. From the hook on the inside wall hung a black-and-white bowling bag, as chic and charmingly inappropriate as everything Chloe did.

For some reason Julia no longer felt the least shame or fear of getting caught. She took down the bag and searched its pockets; did not find what she was looking for; opened Chloe's snakeskin wallet and spread its compartments. There it was, a grey plastic rectangle about the size of a credit card with several round holes randomly punched in one end.

For a moment, Julia wanted to take the money in the wallet, too. But that would just be stupid.

She returned the bag to the locker and gently closed it. From outside the locker room, somewhere down on the courts, came an exuberant yell of victory.

Beer on the floor, tracked by dirty sneakers out of puddles; beer gushing from kegs on rickety tables; beer spilling from plastic glasses balanced on the radiators; beer soaking parts of Julia's t-shirt and her bare arms. She had hated keggers in high school and she hated frat parties now, especially the big ones held in this beautiful old hall that also hosted lectures and religious services.

At the beginning of the year, everyone on her floor, including Chloe and Colton, had gone to these parties. Then they had discovered the bars of the Upper West Side and the clubs of the Lower East. Nowadays, most everyone went off campus on weekends.

But to Chloe Ryder, Manhattan nightlife was old hat. To

hear her talk, she had pretty much taken her first baby steps on the dance floor of Twilo. She considered frat parties, on the other hand, to be ironically cool.

Julia circled the hall, searching. And there they were, all four of them: Chloe, Colton, Chloe's roommate Ramona – a Native American girl who had grown up on a reservation and received full financial aid – and Ramona's Pi Kappa Alpha boyfriend. They were jumping in a circle.

Julia forced her way out of the building. The May night was cool on her hot face. She hit redial on her cell phone. "They're here."

"Gotcha," Haly said. "Either of them leaves, call me immediately, OK?"

"You got it."

Julia sat down on the steps. Gardenia bushes flanked the stone balustrades lower down, and their fragrance enveloped her. She pictured Haly taking the elevator up to the ninth floor – alien territory for her, just as the fourth floor where Haly lived was alien territory for Julia: it even *smelled* different. Nine had once been one of the most cohesive floors, but nowadays they all interacted less. No longer did group study sessions sprawl down the corridor, although that might change again as finals approached. Dan Weiss would be in the lounge – he *lived* in the lounge – and there might be a couple of other people in there watching TV with him. That was a risk. But Chloe and Ramona lived at the other end of the corridor, nearer the elevators than the lounge. Haly would only have to walk a few steps before she could insert the stolen key in the lock of their door. Chloe did not know it had been stolen; she believed she had mislaid it somewhere in their room. She should have reported the loss to campus security, but she expected it would turn up, and in the meantime there was the spare key that Ramona had been issued when she lost hers back during orientation.

Students rollicked up and down the steps. Julia twirled a lock of hair and tried to look detached, not lonely, not a loser. *Losing is not in the Breckinridge playbook.*

Haly opens the door, slips into the room and closes the door behind her. And then? Clips from cheesy movies flickered on the screen of Julia's imagination, none of them remotely plausible. She had, of course, researched magic online, but the only system that appeared to have any widespread credibility was voodoo – and, "Voodoo?" Haly had scoffed when Julia shared her findings. "That's such bullshit. Plus, it's supposed to work at a distance, isn't it? If I knew voodoo I wouldn't need a key to her room in the first place."

"Julia! Oh my God, what are you doing out here?" Chloe plopped onto the steps beside her, blonde hair swinging. "This whole scene is so fucking immature," she said cheerfully.

"I've already had beer spilled on me," Julia said, flapping her t-shirt.

Colton stood on the steep balustrade of the steps and began to walk down it, placing one foot carefully in front of the other.

"Where's Ramona?" Julia said.

Chloe raised her eyebrows. "Oh, she's in there. I think she might be going to have another fight with Greg – he was dancing with some skeezy Barnyard chick. I have to go back in and support her."

"Witness," Colton said, reaching the bottom of the balustrade. He executed a wobbly spin. "I am not drunk." He fell off into the gardenias.

Both girls shrieked. "Oh my God, that was classic," Chloe howled. As Colton rose from the gardenias, she leaned over the steps, threw her arms around him, and planted a smacker on his lips. Previously, scenes like this had filled Julia with hopeless misery. Now she felt calm, assured that there would not be too many more of them. She still did not believe in Haly's purported powers, but she knew one thing for sure: she herself could not go on like this much longer. *Something* was going to give.

"Colt's drunk, and so am I," Chloe said, slinging an arm around Julia's shoulders. The thinness of her frame, her very proximity, made Julia's spine crawl. "Now it's your turn, and don't tell me you've got to go home and studyyyy," she drawled the word mockingly, she who did not need to study to ace every test. "Have you ever even had a hangover? I bet not."

"Yeah, Jules, live a little," Colton said.

Julia's cell phone buzzed. She made a face at them and walked down a couple of steps to answer it.

"All finished," Haly said. "I'm back in my own room. Meiying's not here; d'you want to come over and make s'mores?"

Julia twisted the hem of her t-shirt into a rope. Chloe and Colton staggered arm-in-arm back into the building. They had forgotten about her already. "Oh, why not," Julia said.

"Bellum omnium contra omnes." The professor closed his copy of *Leviathan* and looked up at the class. "What does that mean to you?"

"I think it's like Les Miz."

"Like *Survivor.*"

"Didn't Hobbes ever read Montaigne?" said a plump boy who was cruising for an A. "I mean, didn't he know that tribal societies – what they called savages, didn't they? – live, even back then they lived, in *peace?* With social contracts that were more *durable* than most monarchies? There's no such *thing* as a state of nature."

"Hobbes lived in France, and he's believed to have been familiar with Montaigne. But as we discussed last week, his dark vision of humanity was inspired by the Civil War in England: a war that set neighbors against neighbors."

"Rwanda."

"Northern Ireland."

"The Middle East!"

Julia stared covertly under her bangs at Chloe and Colton. They sat together, as usual, but they were slumped in opposite directions in their chairs. Five days had passed. Was Haly's magic working? Julia could not tell. The discussion veered into contemporary politics. The professor intervened again.

"In Section Four, Hobbes describes a 'kingdom of darkness.' What are some of its characteristics?"

A thoughtful silence fell. This close to finals, even the handful of students who normally dominated the class were behind in their reading.

"Ignorance," Colton said. Julia's heart fluttered with pride in him. "When you don't know the truth – when sh— stuff is being concealed from you. That's when you're in the kingdom of darkness."

"Excellent, Colton. Yes, that—"

"It's like the opposite of freedom of information," Colton concluded.

Chloe twitched.

"Yes, Chloe?"

"I just want to say—" Chloe stared at her desk. Her hands gripped its edge. "I think this class is total bullshit."

Silence paralyzed the room.

"An interesting sentiment," the professor said. He was young, untenured, and now rather pale. "Could you express it in more appropriate language?"

The class tittered.

"No, Mr. Weeny-bird, I could not," Chloe said. "Because you know what, I'm sick of expressing myself appropriately. Actually... actually I only came to this *dump* because it was *appropriate*. I mean I'm Jim Ryder's daughter, maybe it would be more appropriate for me to be a junkie on the club circuit, that's what some people seem to think, but all I ever wanted was to be normal. That's why I came here. Boy was that a mistake. You people – *you people* – " Chloe inhaled, exhaled, blinked. She stood up, pushing her desk away. Its legs scraped loudly. "You think it's so easy being me, well it's not." She plucked at the button of her jeans. "You – you people want to see the scars where I self-harmed for the last ten years? You want to see what it's really like to be Jim Ryder's quote unquote beautiful daughter?"

"Chloe, please." The professor waved his hands. "Please let someone take you to health services…"

"Don't worry about me, dickhead. I'm going." Head high, Chloe stomped towards the door. When she got there, she turned. "I'm going, so you can all get on with your fucking fake-ass shell game!" Her voice spiraled higher. Colton half rose. "And yes, that means you, Colt! *Such* a *rebel*. Spending Daddy's money on weed and E." Her voice trembled with contempt. "Just leave me alone."

The heavy oak door slammed behind her.

Julia looked down at her palms. She clenched and unclenched her hands, leaving nail dents in her flesh. She was breathing hard. *All I ever wanted was to be normal,* she thought.

A girl's whisper carried through the classroom. "Oh my God, I cannot be*lieve* Chloe Ryder is a cutter."

And another whisper: "…weed and E?"

Slowly, every head turned in Colton's direction. He was toying with his pencil, bright red to the roots of his hair.

"**B**ut is it… *true?*" Julia asked.

"It's not as big of a deal as she made it sound. Oh, sure, I may have smoked a couple of joints from time to time. And we may have dropped an E at the Fiji party last month. The brothers were giving them out practically for free. But if that makes me some kind of drug fiend…"

"I know you're not a drug fiend," Julia said hastily. "I mean, I wasn't even shocked. It was just like, whatever."

"Exactly!"

"But I was actually talking about… about Chloe." She mimed fiddling with her jeans button.

"Oh. That." Colton's head drooped. They rounded the lawn where students played lacrosse on sunny days; turned towards their residence hall.

"I'm sorry," Julia muttered. "I shouldn't have asked."

"No. No, I mean, she was the one who fucking told *everyone*. Not like it's my problem, but it was like this deep dark secret for her, you know? I can't believe she just came out

43

with it like… Yeah, it's a real mess. All over here." Colton traced his fingers over his lower abdomen, above his groin. "And here…" Down to the tops of his thighs. Julia shivered. "Seriously nasty. Like, she is *never* wearing a bikini, you know? When I first saw it, I wanted to hurl."

"But you didn't."

"Of course I didn't! Dude, can you imagine? *Bleeaargh.*"

Both of them laughed.

"It was like this huge trust thing for her to let me see them in the first place." They swiped their ID cards at the guard's desk and stepped into the elevator, which smelled of stale pizza. "She's really fragile. It's just an act, her whole happy thing. She really needs…"

"Therapy," Julia suggested.

"She's already in therapy, you didn't know that? I think her therapist is actually damaging her, but whatever, that's another topic. No, she really needs emotional support from like real people. Like you, Jules. I know she trusts you."

"And I'm going to be there for her," Julia said with effusive warmth. "And so are you, right? She's going to need you more than ever now."

"Tell me about it." Colton grimaced. They stepped out into the ninth-floor corridor. The familiar scent of cup ramen and laundry hung on the empty air. Colton hesitated.

Julia plucked up her courage. "I know it must be a burden, Colt. If you need to… I don't know, if you ever need to just let it go for a while. I'm always here."

"Hey, thanks. I totally appreciate that. But I'm OK." Colton made a funny little gesture like a half-salute. "It's not a burden."

"And so I said…" Julia recounted the exchange in a calm monotone. She lay on her back on Haly's bed, gazing up at the ceiling where Haly must have used a stepladder to stick constellations of glow-in-the-dark stars. "Why did I have to be so *obvious?*"

Haly snorted. "Quit reading too much into things."

"You weren't there."

Haly crunched a cookie. She was sitting crosslegged on the floor by the bed with her French text and a box of Chips Ahoy. "I wish I'd been there earlier," she said. "When Little Miss Rockstar went nova. God, can't she even fall apart without turning it into a scene from a soap opera?"

Julia rolled onto her stomach. Face muffled in her folded arms, she said, "I guess that *was*... you?"

"Coincidence would be kind of implausible, huh?"

"It wasn't really what I was expecting."

"Me either. I mean *whoa*. I had no idea."

Julia combed her fingernails through the tassels on the Indian-y cloth that Haly had draped over her desk, which was jammed against the head of the bed. Both this half of the room and the other half had exactly the same configuration of furniture, but they looked as if they had been spliced together by CG. Meiying had a flower-patterned bedspread and tidy stacks of pastel plastic storage baskets. Haly had strewn black clothes all over her half of the floor, decorated the walls with film noir posters, and littered her desk with junk food wrappers and cigarette packets.

Julia sat up. "But Haly, it hasn't *worked*! They haven't broken up, and they're not—"

"Give them time," Haly said.

Julia shook her head. "It's not going to happen," she said wretchedly. "He's gone all saintly. He's got a savior complex. I can't believe I didn't see it before."

"Well, then, that's something else for it to work on. But listen, Jul? Don't take this the wrong way, but he's not a saint. He's just a guy, and he's got track and field practise, hasn't he? And finals coming up. He's got a *life*, and he's too smart to stay in an unhealthy relationship. So..." Haly crunched, swallowed. "I think one more dose should do it." She licked her fingers and held the textbook up to Julia. "Can you quiz me on these verbs?"

Night in the library.

Light gleaming yellow on tables polished by generations of elbows.

Julia looked down at her neatly bulleted and highlighted lists of biology definitions; looked up.

Four tables away, Chloe and Ramona sat within a fort of textbooks, drink bottles, rucksacks, library books, laptops, and looseleaf binders. Ramona scribbled industriously. Chloe sat with her chair pushed back, her head resting on her arm. She appeared to be asleep.

"Haly," Julia whispered.

"Just a minute – what's the difference between spin and handedness?"

"Particles have spin. Molecules are handed. Shouldn't you go?"

"I am never going to pass this test," Haly muttered. She swept her hair back from her forehead. "All right, I'm going."

"You know, I was thinking – why don't you just cast a spell on yourself to be able to do physics? I mean, you're acing all your humanities classes, it seems ridiculous that you can't..."

"Duh, don't you think I would if I could? It doesn't work on me." Haly swept her notes together and stood up. "Same drill, OK?"

She slid between the carrels and out of sight.

With conscious nostalgia for junior high school, Julia drew her name and Colton's inside a heart; erased it. She found a piece of dried gum stuck under the edge of the table and chipped at it with the point of her pencil. She copied the definition of punctuated equilibrium into her notebook. She stared at Chloe and Ramona's backs.

Ramona was no longer writing. As Julia watched, she pushed her chair back and settled her face into the crook of her elbow..

Julia held her breath, as if even from here the noise of an exhalation might wake them. Then she quickly straightened her own and Haly's belongings, arranging them in artfully messy piles so no one else would take their seats, and left the library.

Pulse tripping, she pattered down the steps that took her off campus, hurried along Fraternity Row, then climbed the flight of steps that led straight to the door of their residence hall.

A talk show laugh track greeted her when she stepped out of the elevator, but no one looked out of the lounge. If anyone did, if anyone came out into the hall right now, she would say she was going to visit Chloe – but she reached the door of Chloe and Ramona's unobserved, and turned the handle.

Haly had not locked the door behind her. It opened. Julia stepped in.

In the glare of the room's fluorescent overhead light, which no one ever used, Haly knelt on the floor in front of the closet. Beside her sat a black box with a hinged lid. She was carefully pouring a trickle of something blackish from a vial into a funnel that was connected to what looked like an old-fashioned spectrograph. Another gadget stood on the floor nearby; this one looked like a barometer on a decorative stand made of white marble. All this Julia saw in the split second before Haly's hand jerked, splashing a few drops of the black stuff onto the carpet, and her face came up, terrifying.

Julia recoiled. "It's only me, they're both asleep, I just wanted to see — "

"You can't see!" Haly hunched her body around the gadgets, trying to hide them without taking her eyes off Julia. "Go away, you can't see, you're not allowed!"

"All right, I'm going, I'm going!"

"This is *private!* And you're not doing your job! If we get caught now it'll be your fault!"

"Haly – what *are* those things?"

Haly opened her mouth, closed it, then tipped her head on one side and balanced a finger against one cheek in an exaggeratedly cute pose. "I could tell you but then I'd have to kill you," she said, smiling.

"I'm going." Julia backed towards the door. "I'm going. Look. I'm leaving."

"Go back to the library."

"Yes."

"I'll be there in about twenty minutes."

"Yes." Julia closed the door. The corridor was still empty. Her head felt weirdly hollow and empty.

She could still see Haly moving, twisting around, her knee bumping something on the carpet that rolled: a syringe. And Haly's left sleeve had been rolled up, exposing a Band-Aid on the inside of her arm.

Some months ago Julia and Haly had signed up together for a belly dance class to be held on the campus of the women's college across the street. Expecting to shake their hips, they had been taken aback to find themselves imitating animal noises and "meditating in motion." But it was weirdly fun in a back-to-kindergarten way, and they always went for frozen yogurt afterwards.

Two days after the incident in Chloe's room, Julia turned up at the studio in a state of nervous foreboding, having neither seen nor talked to Haly for twenty-four hours. She could not guess whether Haly would still be mad at her, or pretend nothing had happened. She did not know which she hoped for.

Haly was not there yet. Julia got changed and sat stretching on the floor until class started. Five minutes into their warmup exercises, Haly padded into the studio.

"Hey Haly," Julia whispered, twisting her torso. In the mirror she caught a glimpse of her own pathetically conciliatory smile.

Haly looked straight past her, walked to a spot in the back row, and started to stretch.

"Now, before we begin dancing, let's try something new. I'd like every woman here to laugh with me. Yes, laugh!" The workshop leader, a redheaded woman in a belt of jingling coins, placed her hands on her tummy and let out a series of whoops. Giggles rippled through the room. "That's right! Fake it till you make it! Ha, ha, ha!"

"How, how, how," bellowed the girl next to Julia.

Julia forced out a dubious tee-hee.

"Ha, ha!" laughed Haly behind her. Julia's gaze jumped to the mirror. Haly was doubled over, holding herself, slapping her thighs. Her laughter was so manifestly fake that it made the other girls stare and giggle, then really laugh – and amidst them, Haly roared harder. "Ha ha! HA HA HA!"

After class, Julia fought her way across the changing-room. Haly had not changed out of her sweats and t-shirt. She picked up her bag, stuck her feet into her sneakers, and headed for the door.

"Haly!"

She did not look back.

Alone, Julia wandered despondently back to campus. It was a wet day and her umbrella shed drops on the cobbles of the walks. She had an hour before her next class, but it would be no fun to eat frozen yogurt on her own. Tears pricked her eyes as she realized how much of a difference Haly's company made. "What did I *do?*" she muttered to herself. "It's not *fair!*"

"Jules! Juliaaa!"

Adrenaline jolted through her body. Colton's presence always hit her like a storm, violently knocking down the little edifices of her thoughts. "Hi Colt. Where're you heading to?"

"Chem, but I was gonna grab lunch first."

He had no umbrella; instead he wore a waterproof parka, the hood drawstringed around his face, over baggy shorts and flipflops. His eyelashes were dripping. As they walked on together, Julia tentatively extended her umbrella. Quite naturally, Colton took it from her and held it over both of them. Their sleeves brushed at every pace. Julia's outside shoulder was getting wet, but she scarcely noticed.

"So how's it going," Colton said, "you started studying for finals yet?"

She did not want to talk about her classes, but it was better than silence. The topic of finals took them to the cafeteria in the business school building, through the line, and over to a corner where they dumped their backpacks and sat in the uncomfortable plastic chairs. Julia had a salad. Colton had a chicken sandwich and the frozen yogurt with chocolate syrup and sprinkles that Julia would have got herself, if she had been here with Haly. In between bites, Colton complained about his Chinese class, which was apparently full of Chinese-American kids who had spoken the language with their parents at home. For them it was a soft option.

"Yeah, but everyone's good at something," Julia said. "Like, I'm your typical pre-med; for me that stuff is easy. I mean, I'm taking physics because it's *fun*."

Colton aimed a mock swat at her head. "You are so unnatural. I'm just your typical legacy student, and chem is kicking my butt."

"I could help you study… I mean, if you like."

"Chloe's good at chem. But now…"

Julia's cheeks flamed. She had done it again, overstepped the boundaries of her role in Colton's life. Then she heard what he had said. "But now…?"

Colton squirmed one shoulder and toyed with a plastic knife.

"Colt, what's up? I knew something was going on with you as soon as I saw you." Thinking back, she realized it was true.

"I don't know if I can tell you."

"OK, well…"

"Well, everyone's going to know sooner or later." Colton bent the plastic knife and let it spring back. "Chloe's taking a leave of absence from school."

"She's not even going to stay through finals?" Julia gasped.

"Nope. She says she just can't… oh, I don't know. She never did really explain why she – did what she did, and I don't… you know, it could be something to do with her dad?

But anyway. Yeah. She left this morning." The plastic knife broke in Colton's hands. He was left holding the two pieces of it, his forearms resting on the table. "So that's how it is."

"But you'll stay in touch with her? I mean, you won't..."

"Break up?" He smiled crookedly. "I don't know. Her dad was here. That's one scary dude. He pretty much said he doesn't want me to call or email her."

"But you wouldn't let him..."

"He thinks it's my fault. And hell, maybe he's right, I mean, as far as being with me wasn't helping her. *Obviously* it wasn't, or she wouldn't have..."

Julia whispered, "Started cutting again."

"How did you know?"

"I just guessed."

"Well, yeah. That's what happened. Blood all over the floor. Ramona freaked and called health services."

Colton dug into his frozen yogurt. He ate with gusto, and Julia, watching him, was seized with a sort of awe mingled with fervid tenderness. Without even thinking she reached over and touched the back of his hand. He looked up at her and tried to smile. "Might take you up on that offer," he said.

Julia had to think back to remember what offer she had made. In her mind she had not only offered but promised him everything.

"...So we're studying together, and he was like, 'What are you doing tomorrow tonight?' And I just said nothing special, and then he was like, 'Well, I owe you dinner, so how about Tom's?' And I'm just... oh my God, I can *not* believe this. It's working, it is so totally working, Haly! What am I going to wear?"

"Do you have to sound so surprised? It's, like, not flattering," Haly said into the phone. She exhaled audibly. With exasperated affection, as for the follies of her own childhood, Julia pictured her sitting on the windowsill of her room, ashing her cigarette into the rain. "I told you it would work, didn't I? Surely you never doubted me."

"Well, I have to confess," Julia said archly, "I did have my moments of doubt. Mea culpa."

"That's OK," Haly said. There was a pause. "The question is, now you've got him, what are you going to do with him?"

Julia giggled. A disturbing instinct told her that Haly was not reacting as ecstatically as she should have, that in fact she had not yet forgiven Julia at all (*for what? It was unfair*). But the only thing to do was to pretend everything was all right, and at the moment, that was easy. Julia felt as if all was right not just with her, but with all the birds and beasts and assorted other bio-organisms in the world. "I haven't got him *yet!* We're just having dinner! And he'll probably want to talk about Chloe the whole time."

"Well, let him. But don't encourage him. You don't want to just be the one that he whines to."

"No! Oh, but Haly, what am I going to *wear?* I might have to go shopping."

"For Christ's sake don't do that. You don't want to be like, all suddenly, 'Look, I'm a girl!' Just wear jeans and that nice pink top. Guys love pink."

"Pink top. Check."

"Oh, and Julia…"

"Yeah?"

"Play a little hard to get, huh? Take it from me: if you just give him whatever he wants, he'll end up despising you."

"Oh, Julia."

"Oh, Colt."

"God, you're gorgeous," Colton breathed into her naked breasts. It sounded like a line copied from a movie, but that did not stop Julia from drinking it in. "How come I never noticed how gorgeous you are?"

Because there was always someone more gorgeous in the way, she thought. "And here I thought you liked me for my personality," she said with a shaky laugh.

"I do," Colton said, unfastening her jeans. "Oh, I do."

"Colt, I don't…"

"Stop? You mean stop."

"No, no, I don't mean stop. It's just…" Her body felt floppy; she had drunk a lot. The music from Colton's stereo wheeled around her, and every time he touched her it seemed to sear through the darkness like a stroke of sweet flame. "Don't stop. It's just… uh, I'm a virgin."

"Oh."

"Yeah."

Julia sat up. The unfamiliar smell of boy's room cloyed her nostrils and she needed to escape, but when she stood up, she stubbed her toe on something that rolled. She fell back onto the bed, howling softly. "Ow ow ow."

"Shit, are you OK?"

"My toe; ow ow."

"I think," Colton said with one of the rare flashes of humor Julia loved him for, "I think that might just be fate's way of throwing you into my arms."

Suddenly Julia remembered how convinced she had been, at the start of the year, that making friends with Colton through Contemporary Civilizations was the first step of her destiny; she remembered the agony of dwindling hope and the peculiarly sharp pain of having lost without ever having owned – having lost something that she was about to lose *again*, here, now, through her own insane diffidence.

She turned and kissed him. "There always has to be a first time," she whispered.

"Are you sure?"

"As sure as I'm ever going to be."

She tentatively lowered her hand to the front of his jeans.

In her sleep she heard sirens. Waking with no memory of the sound, she lay and basked in the scarcely credible delight of Colton's arm under her neck, his leg heavy across her thighs. He breathed heavily. She caressed the fine hairs on his forearm and revelled in the mild ache between her legs. She had lost her virginity to the boy she was deliriously in love with. How many girls could say that? It had seemed hopeless, hadn't it? But she had not given up. *Giving up is not in the Breckinridge playbook.*

She could not wait to share her triumph with Haly.

Presently she started to feel too hot; her head throbbed, and she needed the bathroom. With great care she extricated herself from the tangle of Colton's limbs. His roommate, Jeff, had tactfully spent the night elsewhere.

Tiptoeing about the room, she collected her clothes from the floor. She paused by the window and glanced out.

In the sunny morning, two ambulances were parked outside the dorm in Fraternity Row. Paramedics stood around talking with the security guards and a woman who looked like – yes, it was – Sarah Wiseman, the RA from their own floor.

Julia drew back. As she turned from the window, she saw the beginnings of a commotion, the paramedics splitting to clear a path as a stretcher was carried down the steps.

She put on her clothes, gave the sleeping Colton a soft kiss, and hurried down to the bathroom. There were people in the corridor, standing around in knots. Though they must have seen her emerge from Colton's room, they barely seemed to notice her. A worm of anxiety slithered under her breastbone.

Lakshmi, Julia's roommate, was spinning in her desk chair. Julia got the impression she had just been looking out the window.

"Hey, Lakshmi. Uh, hope you weren't worried about me last night?"

"So did you score?"

"Actually, I did," Julia confessed. Lakshmi sat up straight in excitement, but before she could ask any more questions, Julia said, "So what's up, everyone's out in the hall. Did something happen, I mean something *else*?" She rolled her eyes; by now the whole floor knew about Chloe's precipitate departure.

"Oh my God. You haven't heard?"

"No..."

"It's so terrible!"

"What is?" Julia said, starting to feel irrationally angry.

"Well, you're not going to believe this, but it's Ramona. She tried to commit suicide, can you believe it? That's what they're saying. Like, she couldn't handle the pressure of finals or something. But I think it's that room. Like maybe it's cursed!"

The floor seemed to be dropping away from Julia, as if the whole world were an elevator going down too fast.

"She cut her wrists," Lakshmi said, and her excited tone wavered. "Sarah said she's going to be all right. But did you see – oh Julia, did you see how the paramedics were just standing around like they had all the time in the world?"

Julia waited outside the building where they had physics. When she spied Haly's slouching black-clad form, she jumped up and hurried over to her. "I need to talk to you."

"We're going to be late," Haly said, casting an eye at the students streaming into the building.

"We've still got five minutes."

Haly gave her a cold, tough look.

Julia drew on her inner well of righteousness. "Did you know Ramona's dead?"

"Sure. Everyone knows."

"Well, did you know she was going to die?" Julia's voice came out too loudly. A couple of people passing by glanced at her.

Haly did not flinch. She shrugged. "I wouldn't have predicted it."

"But you – you weren't supposed to do anything to *her!*"

"What did you expect? It works on whoever's in range. Like I said, I wouldn't have predicted that Ramona would be so vulnerable. But—" Haly shrugged again. She wandered over to the ornamental hedge, plucked a leaf of privet, and rolled it in her fingers. "Who really knows anyone else? Obviously, she had stuff she was hiding. too."

"You'd know all about *that*," Julia said childishly.

A glint of anger appeared in Haly's dark eyes. "I didn't hide anything from you. I told you the truth."

"You didn't want me to see —"

"But you came snooping after me anyway, didn't you? I didn't want you to see because I knew you'd freak out, and I was right. And now you're blaming me."

"No, I'm not," Julia said. She pleaded, "But why didn't you take your stuff back after – after Chloe?"

"Didn't have a chance, did I?" Haly dropped her crumpled leaf, fumbled in her bag, and lit a cigarette in contempt of the regulation against smoking on the walks. "Not with you out on your *date*."

"If you'd asked me —"

"And defeat the purpose of the whole thing?" Haly shook her head. "I didn't think one more day would make any difference. Oh well. I've got it all back now, anyway: I went and helped Sarah pack up Ramona's stuff last night. Said I was one of her friends."

Julia tried to digest this; gave up. "But Haly, *she* shouldn't have had to die!"

"Excuse me," Haly said. She dragged on her cigarette, brows creasing. "You've got what you wanted. Goal achieved, mission accomplished. What are you so upset about?"

"I —"

"You're supposed to be happy now. Or isn't he that special after all? Was the fun all in the pursuit?"

"He *is* that special, I'm totally crazy about him, but —"

"Well then! Stop complaining. Go away and leave me alone!"

On the last word Haly's voice deepened to a flat growl.

Julia felt as if a bucketful of ice were sliding down her back. She held up her hands in joking surrender and backed away. When she had put some distance between them, she turned and plunged into the building. Down the stairs, down the hall, through the ridiculously tall doors. The auditorium-style classroom was full, the professor already striding around in front of the blackboard. Julia plopped into the first empty seat she came to and dug out her books. She was trembling.

Go away and leave me alone!

Julia had known, without ever having properly under-stood, that Haly was dangerous. Now, clearly the only thing to do, the only way to placate her, was to do exactly as she said. *Leave me alone.* All right, Julia would. (She wouldn't even miss Haly. After all, she had Colton now.) Never again, she vowed to herself, never again, not so much as eye contact...

She applied herself to taking down the scribbles on the blackboard. The door of the classroom whumped, and the back of her neck prickled as someone passed behind her. Glancing under her bangs, she saw Haly drop into an empty seat in the row below.

Another minute passed before Julia dared to look again. Haly had taken out a notebook, but she was not writing. She hunched over her desk, forehead resting on one hand. Her lips moved silently.

Fear liquefied Julia's thoughts. What if Haly were al-ready planning her next campaign, directed against Julia herself?

Haly's shoulders shook; her other hand came up and scrubbed at her nose and eyes. A spark of brightness fell from her face to the desk.

The tension sighed out of Julia's body in one long shudder of relief and sadness. It was all right. Haly was only crying.

IN THE BLACK DESERT

Fifteen minutes before they landed at Cairo, the fat man next to Koji knocked his papers all over the floor.

Koji already resented this man. His thigh, bulgy in khaki, had impinged on Koji's space all the way from Amsterdam. And his work ethic was ridiculous. The guy hadn't watched the inflight movie, had not once stopped scribbling away, writing with a *pen* on pages of looseleaf *paper* – except when he sprawled out to sleep for two hours, imprisoning Koji in the middle seat. At any rate, now his manuscript pages fluttered around Koji's feet, and Koji bent to help scoop them up.

"Ah, thank you. Thank you very much."

"Don't worry about it," Koji said. "What are you writing there, a novel?"

"Well, yes! Yes I am, actually. That's why I'm going to

Egypt. You could call it a research trip." The man smiled, a kind of cringe involving the lower half of his face only. "And yourself?"

"Just a regular working stiff on holiday."

"Alone?"

"Me and my camera. I've got a new one, a digital single lens reflex." Koji indicated the camera bag under the seat in front of him. "Cost me a bundle, but she's got a zoom lens on her like a howitzer. Great autofocus, too, even at ISO 200 – you know, for taking pictures in poor light? Can't wait to try her out on the scenery here."

"Ah yes, the Pyramids," the fat man said vaguely.

Ah no, *not* the Pyramids, actually. Not at any price the Pyramids – silenced by time, smug in their silence, worn down to meaningless nubbins in the mind's eye. Koji wanted to shoot the unfamiliar, the unconventional. Things half buried, the beauty of the neglected. The kind of beauty impossible in Japan, where renewal had all the subtlety of a ton of concrete dropped on your toes, and the land itself conspired to not only bury the past but obliterate it. Third World countries weren't that efficient, thankfully. But all the efficiency the Egyptians could muster would be concentrated around the Pyramids, and so he and his camera would be steering clear, thank you very much.

"I'm Hattori," the fat guy said after a pause.

"Kaneko."

They went through their little ritual of bowing from the neck. Koji could feel their fellow passengers watching them and thinking: *Typical*. The only two Japanese on the flight, and the airline had seated them side by side. It was like a conspiracy. He should've just continued to ignore the fat, scribbling dope for the rest of the flight.

Only a little longer, anyway.

"So what kind of novels do you write, Hattori-san?"

"Oh, well, I'm just a struggling hack..."

Over the next few minutes it became clear that Hattori was not a struggling hack at all. He'd won a small-time literary prize and published five novels, though he couldn't be much older than Koji. He spoke brusquely of these successes, as if embarrassed by them, yet his eyes had a soft, wide-open look that Koji recognized as the mark of the uninjured. Beauty would blossom for this man. Poignant juxtapositions would spring to life before his eyes; girls would smile and joke around with him, colorful old characters would treat him like one of the family, and small animals would come to his hand. The world offers such compensations to the ugly that they actually come out ahead of the game. For all the unfavorable comparisons they have to endure, they benefit from a vast outpouring of pity.

Koji wanted no one's pity, but he would have liked to know what it was to receive something for free – something he actually wanted – rather than having to chase it down.

Then again, Hattori had come an awfully long way in search of what he wanted, too, hadn't he?

"**W**orse in Vietnam! No traffic lights! Here you have!" Koji screeched in English, mentally adding: even if you don't seem to know what they're for.

Embracing his camera bag with one arm, he dug his free hand into the torn stuffing of the seat. Their approach from the airport had been incident-free, but as soon as they wheeled into the center of old Cairo the taxi driver had begun attempting to run down pedestrians, waiting until he scored a very near miss before asking Koji what he thought of Cairo. Now the fellow put on a burst of speed, whipped around another roundabout with another Saddam-like statue in the middle, and hurtled down a narrow street with cars parked on both sides beneath the trees. Koji noticed something. All the cars were facing towards them. "Hey!" he yelled over the peppy Arabic music booming from the radio. "I think this street one way only!"

"What? What?" the driver yelled back.

From between two parked cars a mannequin-like figure lurched, one white rubber boot raised in a goosestep, whitegauntleted arm windmilling. The taxi shot past, missing the figure by a hair's breadth.

"I think that policeman!" Koji howled.

"What? What?"

In the rearview mirror, Koji saw that not only was the driver smiling for the first time since Koji had got into the taxi, he was laughing. Koji started laughing, too. What a fantastic city! When the taxi finally jounced to a halt in front of the Horus Hotel, Koji paid what he was asked for, allowing himself to be gulled out of sheer friendly fellow feeling and exhilaration. Cairo! He could already feel the juices of this place pumping in his veins, and he hadn't even taken out his camera yet.

He spent the next day in the Khan al-Khalili and the older bazaar opposite, photographing a donkey in front of a mosque, women's lacy underwear displayed in bins, women in headscarves fastened with little pearl-headed pins, barrels of cumin and paprika, corncobs lying in puddles, a man carrying a pallet of flatbread on his head, and a stray cat asleep on the seat of a motorbike. Around four o'clock he ponied up to enter the Al-Azhar Mosque. Men knelt praying on the carpeted dais in the atrium, or whatever it was called, while Western tourists milled awkwardly, the women clutching scarves over their hair. An English-speaking guide attached himself to Koji and led him to a flight of dark stone stairs that wound up – and up – and up.

They clambered across the roof and up again to a minaret, where speakers were wired to safety grilles between the elaborately carved pillars of the onion dome overhead. "Now see the Citadel," the guide ordered, pointing into the haze of exhaust fumes that shrouded the city, but Koji was captivated by the roofs nearer at hand. Every rooftop dead flat, every one littered with construction rubble that nobody had bothered to remove, and here an armchair, there a table with its legs in the air, there a bookshelf crammed with books and beside it a low comfortable-looking sofa! He tasted something metallic in his throat. He lifted his camera and began shooting. In a city where it never rains, why *not* leave your bookcase and sofa out on the roof? And more fundamentally, why bother to clear away the leftover bricks when you reach the top of your house, why bother to trim the iron rods that cluster skywards from your support pillars? Indeed, why?

A voice boomed up from the stair. Koji's guide pulled a face.

Like a whale sounding, Hattori emerged from the darkness of the stair.

"Waaa! Kaneko-san! We meet again!"

Today, instead of the offensive khakis and checked shirt he'd worn on the plane, Hattori sported jeans and a cardigan that would have suited a man twice his age.

"Isn't this a splendid mosque? What a view! I hope you're taking lots of pictures!"

Koji nodded, letting his camera slip from his fingers to hang from his neck. He had a dull buzzy feeling in his head, a sense of inevitability. "See?" He pointed. "The Citadel."

"Beautiful, beautiful. How the dome glows in the setting sun," Hattori said absently. His guide was talking in English, his accent too thick and his speech too fast for Koji to follow – he hadn't caught half of what his own guide was telling him, either. Hattori sighed.

"Aren't you taking notes, Hattori-san?" Koji asked.

"Well, you see. This isn't really what I'm after. I mean, one has to do the sights, but I'm mainly looking for – how to put it – incidental color. The kind of thing you can't get out of a guide book."

"Have you visited the Khan al-Khalili yet?"

"Yes, yes, I did that this morning. But I think I may have to get out of Cairo altogether. Off the beaten track." Hattori sighed once more. The sunset reflected brightly on his glasses.

Koji's sense of inevitability clubbed him again. Clearly, he was stuck with this guy. No matter what he did and where he went, Hattori was going to follow in his tracks, like a koi following a man with a bag of bread around a pond. Shamelessly, expectantly, Hattori was waiting for Koji to take pity on him.

This kind of thing had happened to Koji once in college, and a couple of times in his small professional world. It was as if these people knew they couldn't make it on their own, and knew that the Kojis of the world existed to break a trail for them, getting in return – what? A warm altruistic feeling? The satisfaction of a job well done in accord with the laws of nature, which might be imagined to pervade the existence of a camel, a slug, or a stomach bacterium?

Hattori grasped a pillar and hauled himself onto the ledge of the minaret behind the grille. His guide barked angrily. Balancing on tippy-toes, Hattori turned his face to the polluted wind. "Waaa!" he hooted. *"Splendid* view!"

And yet, Koji thought, and yet… "Hey, Hattori! You'd better come down from there." When the flushed writer had complied, Koji continued, "By the way, I've hired a driver to take me to the desert tomorrow. We're going to camp out under the stars. You want to come along? Cheaper that way for both of us."

Hattori's eyes vanished in a grin. Koji didn't need to hear his answer, and that was just as well, for at that moment the speakers around the minaret exploded into action, calling on all to kneel, bawling out the way to Mecca, the path of salvation.

"So what do *you* do, Kaneko-san?"

The jeep's stereo was oompahing, and Koji pretended he hadn't heard, but when Hattori repeated the question louder, he had to reply. "I'm a journalist."

"Oh! Seriously?"

"Ever read *Manga Metro?* I write scripts for them." Cults, kidnappings, murders, celebrity dramas, Koji's job was to punch them up, work the raw news into storylines with the maximum nudity and/or violence for the inhouse artists to get their chops into. *Manga Metro* was for people who did not read newspapers, never opened a book. "I do some freelance work for the regular tabloids, too."

"Really! Excellent!"

"You're embarrassing me," Koji simpered. He couldn't resist twisting around in the front seat to get a sight of Hattori's face. The combination of disappointment, contempt, and discomfort was priceless.

"Well, I've always said we have to get the younger generation reading by any means necessary." Was this really the best Hattori could do? Probably. "I'd much rather see them reading *Manga Metro* than, you know —" He mimed pushing buttons with his thumbs.

"Me, too. Hey, I've got to pay the rent!"

"You probably make more than I do!" Hattori laughed, visibly relieved to have found a way to humble himself before Koji again.

Outside, the desert slid past, endless sandbanks coated with black gravel, as if the topmost layer had been fused to glass and then smashed into a billion pieces.

One oasis, several roadblocks, and a range of ferrous hills later, they veered off the highway into the desert. The jeep's 4x4 drive made quick work of the black-speckled sand. Around them, bulbous sculptures of white rock sheered up against the evening sky, their bases scooped out by the wind. "The White Desert," said the driver. Koji took pictures.

Malouf, their driver and guide, was a Bedouin. He had seemed to be a taciturn man, but when he witnessed the sight of Hattori trying to put up the tent that had been procured for him, he laughed so hard that he had to stalk around in circles, waving his hands. Then he took over. Koji already had his tent up by that time and was wandering around the area they'd chosen to camp in, taking more pictures.

The rock formations impressed themselves hard on the lens. By silhouetting them against the dying light, Koji could transform them into dinosaurs, monstrous toadstools, the hulls of ancient boats gone down in this trackless sea – but weren't these just cheap tricks? In spite of himself he was turning the unexpected fractal beauty of this landscape into postcards; punching it up. To shoot it as it really was, he needed to locate something transient in it – its soul. It would not give itself to him.

He returned to the campsite, where Malouf had started a fire and was chopping vegetables for a stew. Koji and Hattori fed the fire the thorny dead branches of scrub and talked inconsequentially of politics. It was pretty much the same conversation Koji had every time he went out drinking with his coworkers. In Tokyo these topics reliably suffused him with rage, but now he just found himself getting depressed. It was this sense he had that Hattori was humoring him. At first, the writer had been eagerly sociable, but now he knew what Koji did for a living, it was as if he'd decided after all not to waste on him any of the insight and original thought that he (presumably) put into his books.

On the other hand, maybe Hattori didn't have an insightful bone in his body. Maybe he was a honking great fraud. This would have been a comforting reflection if Koji could have made himself believe it.

Darkness had fallen by the time the stew was ready. As they ate, Hattori kept glancing away from the fire. Malouf laughed. "Oh, you see Mr. Fox!"

"What?" Koji said. "Who?"

"A fox, a desert fox," Hattori burbled. Lumbering to his feet he made for the edge of the campfire's circle of light. Eyes flashed green, low to the ground. Koji reached for his camera. Hattori flung a crust of flatbread. The eyes vanished.

"He come back after!" Malouf said. "He come back and take your shoes!"

"In Japan," Koji said to Malouf, having to refer to Hattori for some of the English words, "foxes have magical powers. Sometimes they can transform themselves into human beings." A stroke of excitement hammered his heart as he remembered those flashing green eyes.

"Japan is a long way from Egypt, yes? I am from Farafra. When my father was young, he take five days to reach Cairo by riding on camel. Now we driving by jeep in five hours!" Malouf smiled and shrugged. He reached into his pack, took out a complicated glass flower vase, fitted tinfoil over its finial. "You like hookah?"

Hattori said he didn't smoke, but Koji accepted. After seeing the fox, he was up for anything. The writer retired into his tent. Koji and Malouf sat over the dying fire sucking on the hookah and talking about Japan, Egypt, the desert, legends and ghost stories of their childhoods. Koji suspected that apple-flavored tobacco was not all the Bedouin had put into the tinfoil cup; by the time he wobbled off to his tent, the night was wheeling around him and his vision had switched to single-shot mode, so that things appeared to him as a series of still frames: stars – *click*. Bootlaces – *click*. Sleeping-bag – *click*.

He lay on his back with his head out of his tent. Malouf lay bundled in rugs between the dying fire and the crude, incongruous silhouette of the jeep. It had grown cold, but Koji did not feel it. Overhead blazed a million unimaginably distant suns; he framed them in his fingers. *Click.*

Maybe it was the fox that woke him.

Struggling out of his sleeping-bag, he shivered. A chill wind had picked up. He stumbled around behind the nearest formation and pissed a dark hole in the sand. The stars had vanished. The moon floated overhead, almost full. His head was clear.

He went back to his tent, got his windbreaker and his camera. Eerie, achromatic, the moonlight bathed the rock formations, the jeep, and Malouf's sleeping form. The flap of Hattori's tent hung open. The writer was not inside. Koji couldn't see him anywhere, but he could see the pawprints of the fox curving away from the campfire. He photographed the tracks, then followed them.

Some distance away from the campfire, he spotted Hattori's cumbrous silhouette. The fox had led Koji in the right direction. Hattori was moving in a near-crouch, playing a torch on the ground, stooping now and then to pick something up. Koji strolled right up to him before Hattori noticed him. "Oh! Kaneko-san! What do you think of this moonlight? Back in Tokyo, we almost forget the moon exists, huh?"

Koji's irritation, which had been stealing away under the tidal pressure of the moonlight, returned full force at this reminder of the man's talent for marvelling at the obvious. It was probably just Hattori's way of trying to get on Koji's level, not intimidate him by talking in high-flown writerly language. If so, he had no idea what it took to intimidate Koji, which was a shame but only to be expected. But on the other hand, maybe Hattori was sincere. Maybe he saw more in the obvious than Koji did. Maybe he fully, continuously, and joyfully apprehended that fleeting value of beauty which Koji could capture only after the fact, when dwelling on his most successful photographs, which were usually the spontaneous ones he composed by instinct...

But no; that was giving the fat guy way too much credit.

"What are you grubbing up there?"

"These! Oh, it's just amazing. Let me show you." Hattori opened his pudgy fist and shone his torch on the flat of his palm, where several small black and brown seashells lay. "Can you believe it? Fossils! Or are they encased in iron – magma? I don't know when there was last volcanic activity here. I'll have to look that up. But they look like pyrites, don't they? See, they're actually rusting! Rusted seashells! Who'd ever have thought it. Hundreds of miles from the sea..."

Koji bent down to inspect the black gravel that littered the sandbank where they stood. It lay in drifts, he now saw, as if deposited by waves. It was *all* fossils.

"There are a lot of other interesting bits and pieces, too. Like this one. See its odd shape, it's not a seashell. It looks like a geodesic crystal. All these little points. What on earth could have caused such crystals to form...? Oh, if only I were a geologist!"

Koji wanted to laugh. Picking his words carefully, he said, "Hattori-san, we were driving past this stuff – we were driving *over* it for hours. Couldn't you have picked some of these up yesterday? Why now, in the middle of the night?"

Hattori looked bewildered. "Well – as a matter of fact, I only just noticed... I came out for a walk and saw them in the light from my torch. Shells and crystals. Yesterday, I thought it was all just gravel. But look!" He held his hand out. "Aren't they beautiful!"

"I'll show you something beautiful," Koji said, and he swung his camera into Hattori's face. The fat man tipped over backwards with an astonished *ungh*. Before he could rise Koji was on him, crouching astride him, battering his face with the heavy metal-bodied digital single lens reflex, and it was beautiful, so beautiful that he was crying. Hattori's limbs jerked and danced; ineffectually he struck at Koji's legs. For a while he tried to speak, to plead for mercy, but that ended when Koji reduced his mouth to a bleeding pulp. Next it was the turn of his eyes. Tears ran down Koji's own face as he pounded them with the handle of Hattori's own torch. Tears of salt and tears of blood mingled and flowed into the sand, into the dried bed of that prehistoric sea.

He thought for some reason that Hattori would be hard to kill, but the writer stopped moving quite soon, and stopped breathing a couple of minutes after that. Perhaps the crushing of his nose had driven bone splinters into his brain. Koji had written a script once in which the murder victim died in that way.

He sniffled; stepped back; stooped again and wiped his hands on Hattori's jeans. Then he fearfully examined his camera. Its body was dented, and the lens no longer fastened quite flush, which might be a problem, but the screen lit up when he turned it on, and the functions all worked. Way to go, Japanese technology!

He cleaned the lens on Hattori's shirttail, then straightened up and focused on the corpse. It was a shame he hadn't brought his tripod. Oh, well. He started circling the corpse, taking pictures.

A NATURAL PHENOMENON

The dolmen felt sticky to the touch. Kathryn drew back her hand. There was a speckly brownish residue on her fingers. She wiped them on her jeans and walked around the outside of the granite uprights to Colm, who stood beside their rented car, looking down at the town of Kilcoole.

"Trying to imagine this place a hundred years ago," he said. "I think my head might explode."

Kathryn had been thinking of eras much longer ago than that. But she nodded. "It's hard to imagine why anyone would ever have wanted to leave."

"Oh, I don't know." Colm's laugh was strained. "I think I want to leave already."

"Come on, Colm, jeez. We knew it wasn't going to be all shamrocks and leprechauns."

"No, of course not, but when you've got this really – really strong connection to someplace —"

"Then OK, maybe it is a bad idea to go there in real life," Kathryn said tartly. "And maybe we wasted our vacation, and we should just go and hide out in a freaking Holiday Inn for the rest of the week."

Face set, Colm shook his head. "You don't get it."

You don't get it! The refrain of their five-year relationship, Colm's preferred way of ending a conversation when he could not be bothered to explain himself, or was simply feeling lazy – for Colm was lazy, and pessimistic, in Kathryn's opinion, a bad combination that threatened to turn his life into a string of self-fulfilling prophecies.

He had hit the stock-options jackpot on his first job out of school. After that he had drifted from Santa Clara to Austin, from Austin to Asheville, from Asheville to Boston, his period of dormancy growing shorter each time, like a serial killer's intervals. During this slow migration Kathryn had almost unintentionally cultivated a habit of pretending not to get it, even when she partially or entirely did. To her fell the task of mustering sufficient insensitivity to keep their relationship functioning.

"Well, I'm hungry," she said, "and thanks to the new! now with more imported groceries Ireland, we've got Greek salad, Polish sausage, Australian wine, and some French bread that looks improbably like the real thing. Let's find out how it tastes, whaddaya say, hombre?"

They spread out their picnic on one of the rain ponchos they had bought in Galway, next to the dolmen, in its shade though not actually beneath its massive roof.

They had come to Ireland on a whim, following a cash windfall, to trace Colm's roots. His grandparents on both sides had emigrated from the district around Kilcoole.

Kathryn had not expected that at the height of summer, the south of Ireland would be as hot as the Mediterranean. Even up here the day was windless. They had been able to drive to the very top of the hill and park on the grass beside the dolmen that seemed as uncared-for as it was unvisited, despite its prominence in their guidebook. Below the adjacent cattle field, Kilcoole tumbled steeply to a stone-walled harbor. Inland, the town had bloated into a traffic-infested snarl of new housing estates, competing gas stations and car dealerships, and the Tesco where they had bought their lunch before driving up here – this was the vista that had depressed Colm so much.

But when they first drove across the causeway, towards the old town straggling to meet them in pastel ragtag, while seagulls swooped screaming, Kathryn had exclaimed aloud, "*Yes!* Oh Colm, can't you just see us living here? We could telecommute…" This, surely, was what Colm had been looking for all these years. But their excitement had faded into disappointment as they discovered that the old town was just a façade nowadays.

Now she said aloud, "It's just a question of perspective." Colm did not respond, but chewing on her baguette sandwich, she applied her mind with more urgency than usual to the problem of their future.

The birds got most of the baguette, the Polish sausage went back into the car; the Australian wine did its work. Side by side, in the shade of the dolmen, they went to sleep.

"Yes! *Yes!*"

Kathryn raised herself on one elbow. Colm lay flat on his stomach, taking pictures of the sunset that now swamped the top of the hill. Burnished spears of light glanced off his lens. "Yes! Wow!" He scrambled up and retreated from the dolmen. "Kath, can you stand in between – yeah – let me see your profile – yeah!"

She draped herself sexily against the bulkier of the upright slabs; arched her back and thrust out her pelvis in homage to an image from some advertisement floating around in the bilge of her brain. Colm had confessed to her once that he'd first been attracted to her "aesthetically," and she sometimes thought that might still be his main reason for staying with her. Still, it was nicer to be appreciated than not.

"God, you're gorgeous," he muttered. *Click, click.* The ends of her hair tickled the small of her back where her baby tee had ridden up. Something dripped on her forehead and slid down between her eyes.

"Eek!" She swiped the back of her hand across her forehead; stared at it aghast. "I'm bleeding. Colm!"

"What? Lemme see. What did you do?"

"Nothing – I just—"

"You're not even scratched. Where'd that come from?"

As they stared up at the roof of the dolmen, blackness welled in a shadowed crevice, bulged, and fell sparkling into Colm's palm. It filled the crease of his head line, bright red.

"Oh my God." He fumbled for his camera. "Here, take it—" He ripped the strap over his head and thrust it out to her. "I already put it on video mode. Just keep shooting."

"Something must be dead up there," Kathryn moaned. Her hands were shaking, and Colm would later bewail the jerkiness of the video that showed a drop of liquid welling out of the granite overhead, then splashing into his cupped hands. But even so, the color of the liquid spoke clearly enough; and there was nothing on top of the dolmen, nor if there had been, any way for its blood to seep through the stone.

"Jaysus," said Maura O'Brien. She sat on the sofa in her "front room" at the Harbor View B&B, looking at the screen of Colm's camera, while the two Americans stood expectantly on either side of her.

"It's gotta be a natural phenomenon," Colm said.

"We think it may be the explanation for all those bleeding statues of saints," Kathryn said. "I mean, whatever the explanation is."

"I'd say the explanation is that someone's been playing a trick on you," Maura said. "How long did it go on like that? When did it stop?"

Kathryn resented her for pouring cold water on Colm's excitement, but Colm did not notice. He said eagerly, "It started when the sunlight hit the underside of the rock – which means the sun was pretty low – and it stopped when the sun went down. I mean, that's the interesting thing, isn't it? It's like Newgrange or something!" Catching himself at last, he made a rueful grimace. "I mean, I guess we've probably been played – tricked, but good. But I can't see how they did it."

"Neither can I," Maura said, handing the camera back to him. "Sure I don't think I'd want to know." She was in her fifties, thin, with a spongy white face. She rose and straightened her hooded sweater. "But there's people desperate to believe all this kind of thing, isn't there? Send that video into the television, you could be famous!" She smiled, exposing the missing canine that had given Kathryn a shock when they first met. "Will you be going out again for supper? I can recommend you a local restaurant."

Given the rise of the euro against the dollar, they were avoiding restaurants. "We thought we might just go for a drink," Colm said vaguely.

"Ah, then maybe I'll see you at Houlihan's later. Tell Diarmid you're staying at the Harbor View, anyway."

"Now we know which pub to avoid," Kathryn muttered to Colm when they were out of the room.

But they soon discovered that Houlihan's was the only game in town. There were four other pubs dotted along the streets that forked up from the harbor, with light coming from behind their frosted glass windows; but all of their front doors were locked shut.

After the last of these disappointments, they circled back to walk along the harbor. The only other people out in the pleasantly cool evening were a party of possibly German tourists. They were approaching each other, both groups making preliminary sideways jinks, when running footsteps hurtled down the hill.

A young man burst into view, flailed to change direction, and flung himself along the sidewalk towards them. Fair and spotty, maybe sixteen, he had a blank, strained look on his face. Only afterwards would Kathryn recognise it as the look of terror. Colm held out an arm. The boy gasped out something that was not English and leapt off the curb to get past them. Spinning, they watched him vanish around the next corner. His footsteps receded up the town's other street. A moment later a big silver Jeep roared down the hill, slewed heavily, and turned the same corner.

"Shit!" Colm exclaimed, eyes bright.

"This place is dangerous," the largest of the German tourists shouted at them. "Too many Poles."

"You wanted Europe, you got Europe," Colm muttered, too late for it to be a riposte, as the Germans vanished into La Mouette seafood restaurant. "Shit."

"More like the fucking Bronx," Kaitlin said loudly. Rigid, she waited for the gunshots; but of course no sound came except for the fading purr of the Jeep's engine and the lapping of the waves on the harbor wall.

"Do you want to go back to the B&B?"

"Well, if—"

"I can walk you back and then go for a drink by myself."

"No. No, let's just find this goddamn Houlihan's and – and get wrecked. We deserve it."

"Diarmid!" the bartender called to a bearded young man sitting farther down the bar. "Couple of Maura's guests here."

"Cheers," the young man said. He had shiny, ratty eyes, and Kathryn knew how he would have looked at her if Colm were not there. "Enjoying yourselves?"

"My grandparents emigrated from Kilcoole," Colm said. "I'm Colm; this is Kathryn."

"American, are you?"

"Yes," Colm said.

"And we're starting to think there's no real difference between Ireland and the States," Kathryn said, still speaking too loudly. She described their odd encounter on the waterfront, trying to present it as a funny story but failing.

"I'd say that was the travellers. There's a whole tribe of them up in the new estate, it's a serious problem." Diarmid slipped off his barstool and headed for the back door. Colm and Kathryn followed him. The moment they were clear of the threshhold, he pulled out a packet of Marlboros and lit up, contributing to the clouds of smoke that tainted the evening. The courtyard was full of rawboned men and vivid women sitting with pints and cigarettes at picnic tables surmounted by Heineken umbrellas. Diarmid nodded around at them, then returned his attention to Colm and Kathryn. "Ireland's a very different place from what it used to be, you know. Try to buy a holiday cottage down here, it'll set you back half a million euros."

"That's crazy!" Kathryn said. The morning's daydream of relocation seemed boundlessly stupid to her now.

"Sure, this isn't the richest country in Europe, it's only the most expensive."

"You're not kidding," Colm said, grinning. "The Celtic tiger —"

"There never was a Celtic tiger. Only the EU's big fat tit."

Colm laughed, charmed, and Diarmid winked at him. There was something mocking in the man's expression, Kathryn thought. She was maybe over-sensitive, remembering the facile and friendly rebuffing they had gotten in previous pubs in previous towns, which did not quite amount to anti-Americanism, but felt like a related species of contempt. Diarmid was playing with Colm as a bored man might play with a paperclip. Of course Kilcoole was no different. It had been silly and romantic of her to hope for anything else. Oh *screw* them, she thought angrily, screw them all, and in her mind the dolmen wept – drip, drip, drip.

"**K**ath! Kathie!"

She had come back to the B&B alone in the end and toppled into bed, she could not say how many minutes ago. Colm pinned her beneath the heavy slab of sheets and blankets, kissing her cheek and ear. "I shouldn't have let you leave on your own. Thank God you're OK." His breath reeked of Guinness and cigarettes.

"Oh baby, just lie down."

"Can't, Diarmid and the guys are waiting for me." He hauled her into a sitting position. "Look. Up there. Open your eyes, Kath."

Their room was dark; outside the window, beyond the roofs, white beams flickered against the sky. "What's that?"

Flashlights moving on the hilltop. Halogen beams. They pulsed on and off irregularly, half hidden behind dark shapes like trees, and then one massive pulse revealed the roof of the dolmen. The beams sprayed up like a fallen aurora behind that granite frame, a door to nowhere. "Call the press, hombre, it's a UFO," Kathryn said in her bad Spanish accent. A sickening pang slid through her head, and she closed her eyes, wincing. "You're not really going back out, are you?"

"I told them…"

"Fine, then, go on. I don't care." Her head pulsed in time with the unseen flashes of white fire.

Pause. Then, "Oh Kath, I'm such an asshole. Do you forgive me?"

This at least was familiar, the penultimate chord of their sad ballad of mutual resentment. Kathryn sighed. "I'm sleepy," she pleaded. "Yes, of course I forgive you…" Disappointment with him, with the world, bit deep inside her like acid. "If you're really sorry, lie down and go to sleep. I've got a thumper already, the real McCoy."

"Like they say, be careful what you wish for," Colm mumbled, flopping into bed beside her. He cast off all the covers; she dragged them back; he lay on his face, head buried in the crook of one arm. Kathryn was drifting off to sleep again when she realized he was crying.

"Colm! Baby, what's wrong?" (He could always get to her with tears.)

"I gotta get out of here."

She exhaled hard. "Go on, then. Don't let me stop you."

"I mean, out of this town."

"We're leaving tomorrow."

"But it's no good now. I guess I always knew… This is what I really am. This…" The last words dissolved into a quiet sob.

"What?"

"I'm going to lose you."

She half sat up. "You aren't going to lose me unless you dump me, hombre. Not unless you want to."

"Doesn't matter if I want to or not." His sobs turned into wet laughter. She flinched.

"Don't," she said at last. "Colm, don't keep putting us through this. Go to sleep." Stiffly, she placed her arm over his back.

She was asleep even before she could ascertain by his breathing that he had stopped crying.

She woke again and she was alone and it was still dark. She leaned on the windowsill, whispering to herself to calm down. Her head still throbbed, but it barely intruded on her attention. On the hilltop, the lights had gone away – no, they hadn't. As she watched, a single beam flicked on and then off, on and off again.

A signal.

She struggled into her clothes, tiptoed downstairs, and eased out of the B&B, freezing for a second when the mail slot clanked, allowing the door to relock behind her. She paused to reorient herself, then turned and hurried up the hill past the terrace of conjoined houses. The dim yellow glow of the streetlights dulled their cheery colors and cast shard-like shadows on their windows, making them look as if they had been abandoned for a hundred years, and that was spooky, but when she reached the top of the terrace, the darkness closed around her, and that was worse. Things rustled in the hedgerows. She advanced without a cry, without a whisper.

At last the hedge on her right fell away, the scent of manure from the cattle field faded, a breath of wind touched her face, and she was on the hilltop.

Turning, she saw the town below her, the clustered lights running out into the grid of the new development. The dolmen rose blackly between her and the view. In the shadows at its feet nothing moved.

She took a step forward. "Colm?"

Flash. Shadows scurried away, and for that split second she saw the uprights of the dolmen splashed with blood, gore dripping from the roof. But in her mind what lingered was the shadows humped around the uprights, some of which had not been so quick to flee that transient glare of white light. Some of them had limped, some dragged themselves away on smashed legs. Some had crawled.

She stuffed her knuckles into her mouth, biting back a scream. Yet she kept going, shuffling wide around the dolmen, the dewy grass licking her ankles. "Colm?"

Only the cry of a bird answered her. A crow, she thought; no, a raven. It sounded as if it was sitting on top of the dolmen, which now lay slightly behind her and to her left.

"Don't look," she whispered to herself.

"Kathryn." It was a murmur, barely more than the rustle of wind in grass. With the greatest difficulty she stopped herself from turning to face it.

"Don't look back."

"Colm came looking for himself. Won't you look for yourself, too?" The voice wheedled obscenely in her mind. "G'wan, just one little peek…"

She knew it would be death to glance back. She pressed forward, every step a victory over her own terror, until she reached the very edge of the grassy hilltop. Here, she remembered, the land fell away in a welter of gorse to the top of the cattle field. She could go no further, and so here she sank down, her eyes fixed on the streetlights below, so near and yet a world away. Beyond the lights spread the infinite blackness of the sea; even that seemed closer.

The dew dampened her and still she sat. The darkness

grew paler, and still she sat. Eventually the first ray of sunrise shot over the hill behind her. She had no excuse not to turn around then.

Shading her eyes, she knew what she expected to see: Colm's broken body laid beneath the dolmen. But the red morning sunlight shone only on grass.

Limply puzzled, she sank back to the ground, letting out a dry little laugh that did not sound like her own.

Distant traffic fractured the morning silence. One engine was coming closer. Its serrated rumble approached up the hill. Kathryn waited. She expected the silver Jeep; but she was wrong again. The vehicle that climbed from behind the hedges was a black SUV with tinted windows. It pulled over behind the dolmen and sat idling noisily. Kathryn lurched to her feet.

The near passenger door thunked back. She saw several pairs of jeaned knees in the shadowed interior. Colm clambered over them and jumped out. He waved to Kathryn, turned and said something to the driver of the SUV, then slammed the door. As he waved the vehicle off, he swayed, lost his balance and took a staggering step.

Kathryn flew to him. "Baby! Where the hell – who the hell—"

Colm shrugged off her supportive arm. "I didn't expect to see you here," he said, not quite peevishly. "I was just going to watch the sunrise and then go back to the B&B."

"Well, we can watch the sunrise together," Kathryn said with awful fake cheerfulness.

But it was him she watched. There was something in his eyes she did not recognize, or an absence of something she did. The look he got when he was hiding something from her; it was not there. In its place, a strange limpidity. The grass still sparkled with dew; Colm grimaced at it; they both stayed standing. The sun rose inexorably above the hill.

At last Kathryn could stand it no longer. "Where've you *been?*"

"Up here. Out there. Around." He looked down at his

hands. Following his gaze, she saw that his fingernails had black rims, they were clogged with something dark.

"Yeah, and?"

He pursed his lips, looking canny and, momentarily, very Irish. Then he grinned widely at her. "You know, you were right. I can really see us both staying here forever."

THE FOREST OF SINCERITY

I gatecrashed my boyfriend's funeral. His family had hired an upstairs room at an ornate, yellowing hotel in eastern Tokyo. The black attire of the mourners soaked up the light from the chandeliers. Their voices fuzzed out the lite classical Muzak. In this cocktail-party atmosphere, I didn't feel too conspicuous, though I was the only gaijin present.

I snagged a drink from the buffet and stood in a corner. Flowers and gold drapery smothered the shrine at the far end of the room. Shrine? Bier? Altar? Somewhere in there lay as much of Shunji as they'd managed to scrape up from the street. Bad mental images there. But of all things, it was the shrine's photographic backdrop that really creeped me out. A view of a mountain peak, backlit as if the sun was setting behind it, and down from its bony shoulders swept a mantle of forest so dense and dark that you could practically smell the pine needles rotting on the ground. A generic mountain. It couldn't be Fuji-san from any angle. It was a stock shot taken somewhere in the Japanese Alps – and so Shunji's parents didn't know, I told myself. How could they? They'd probably just chosen the picture because Shunji had been nuts for mountain climbing as a college student. Either that, or the hotel staff had picked it without consulting them. All the same, it made me wish I hadn't come. I hated coincidences.

I abandoned my drink in a rubber plant and started through the crowd. At the front of the room, a hunchbacked old lady lit incense and jammed the sticks into the urn before retreating to the row of folding chairs before the shrine. I was going to offer incense, too. Let them try and stop me if they liked, and then we'd have a nice little scene.

Keeping an eye out for Shunji's parents, whom I wanted to avoid, I bumped into someone and apologized in Japanese.

"Lily?"

He knew my name, but I didn't recognize him.

"Too bad about Shunji. I thought he, if anyone, was going to be OK. You know?"

"He *was* OK," I said, stung. "Better than OK." I started to speak about Shunji's job at Takada Industries, his belated metamorphosis from slacker into salaryman. Then I stopped, since I still didn't know who I was talking to. The skinny build and longish hair offered a whiff of otaku, but no other clues. When I checked out the knot of guys he'd been standing with, none of them met my eyes. So, he wasn't actually with them. He'd just been dawdling near them to hide the fact that he'd come alone – like me.

My pulse picked up. I knew there was no one left of the core group. But a number of people had come along with us once or twice, forming no real connections and never heard from again, except online. Anyone like that would be here alone, and I might not recognize them immediately. It had been four long years since Bu-taro's death put us out of business.

"I guess it just goes to show," the guy said, shaking his head in a faux worldly manner. "You don't have to have money troubles or a broken heart; you don't have to be disturbed or even depressed…"

"Shunji didn't kill himself," I said. "He *fell.*"

Ghoulish curiosity animated the guy's face. "So why do you think he was up on the roof in the first place?"

If only I knew! But I knew what the guy wanted to hear, all right. Just this morning I'd been reading through posts by more of our friends that interpreted Shunji's death as yet another coverup, and there was no law that said I had to deal with this kind of thing at his *funeral.* I gave the guy a wounded glare and turned away without another word.

Plunging through the crowd, I came face to face with Shunji's sister. As we hugged, I realized I was trembling. "It's an amazing turnout, isn't it?" Natsume said with a watery smile. "Nice for Mom and Dad, but they're a bit overwhelmed… Sorry."

"That's OK. Which ones are they?"

She pointed furtively, then said in an outburst of passion, "Who *are* all these people, anyway? We haven't got enough attendance presents… He was always so extroverted, but I never knew he had *this* many friends!"

"Well, let's see," I said. "He switched jobs eight times between graduation and landing the gig at Takada. That's a lot of connections. And some of this lot probably never met him face to face at all. They just —"

"It wasn't on the news. It makes you think, doesn't it? How many people die and it never gets onto TV?"

"No, but it's all over the communities that he used to post to."

Not listening, she clutched my arm. "Mom would really like to meet you. I mean, not *today*, that would be too awkward, but maybe in a few weeks…"

I glanced at the lacquered elderly woman that Natsume had pointed out. She was laughing and chatting with a group of older guests. Laughing and chatting, at her son's funeral.

"She was saying that she regretted never having had you over…"

"Well, it's a bit late for that, isn't it?" As soon as I'd spoken, I looked away from Natsume's big glittering eyes, ashamed of myself. She didn't know why her parents had disapproved of my relationship with Shunji, any more than I did. It might have hinged on our refusal to get married. That piece of paper means a lot more in Japan, as I'd learned when the police called Shunji's parents instead of me, and so did his employers, even though I was listed as emergency contact. There was also the eldest son thing, as my friends had pointed out. I would have been first in line to take care of Shunji's parents when they got helpless with age, and if that was what was on their minds, I couldn't blame them for going into denial. They shouldn't have judged me without meeting me, of course. But what use were second thoughts now? What use were kind gestures? The future momentarily closed in on me like a black tunnel. Shunji was dead, and I – well.

Shunji's mother had noticed my absentminded stare. Our eyes met for a second, and then she was moving sideways, putting more people between us.

I said to Natsume, "Can I ask you something. Who chose that picture on the shrine? Your mom? Your dad?"

"It's just his college graduation photo–"

"I mean the…" Cunningly, I didn't say *the forest.* "The mountain."

"I think it was just part of the package," she said.

From across the room came the crash of glass hitting the floor. I whispered to Natsume that I would email her. The smell of incense lingered on the stairs, lending morbidly ecclesiastical associations to the chimes from the front desk and the elevators.

I'd said nothing at work, although I was aware that the longer I waited, the harder it would be to tell anyone.

Shunji had died on Wednesday night and now it was Friday night. Customers milled around the high tables and performed air guitar solos on the little dance floor, the usual mix of metalheads with scraggly long hair and former metalheads in suits. Yen notes banked up in the register like leaves blown off a tree, damp to the point of decomposition from my perpetually wet fingers. Kiyoko, the assistant bartender, and I plonked down rows of dripping shots, Coronas with juicy eighths of lime in their necks, and long icy cocktails in glasses that immediately turned opaque in the humidity. Murata-san festered at his end of the bar. Our troglodyte commander-in-chief, the owner of Axez, he was the scowling Ringlord of the bass-heaviest sound system in Kabukicho and a CD collection to match. Black Sabbath, Iron Maiden, Pantera, Metallica... Sandman, oh Sandman, come and take me away.

Though biased in favor of American hard rock and heavy metal, Murata-san had a few Japanese bands in his collection, including Haramatikk. I knew it was coming sooner or later, but it still shook me when the opening chords of their first hit ripped out of the speakers. Nowadays, they're signed to Sony, but six years ago they were just another gang of struggling shredders, with one big advantage over their peers: Shunji, a high school buddy of their bassist. He set up a gothtastic website for them, which I discovered when I was still an English teacher. By that time, the chatter on the site's forum had already sprawled away from heavy metal; and soon Shunji introduced a new board for Other Topics. Anyone could access it, but you had to register to post. Eventually, the core membership of Other Topics leveled off at just seven people: Bu-taro, Ninnik, Egg, Maedaza, Kott-san, Shunji (aka Makutive), and me (aka Suzuran, which means "lily of the valley," and later I wished I'd chosen any other name).

I was more of a mascot than a real member of the group, at least to begin with. The inaugural JuKyo expedition happened unknown to me, a few weeks before I met Shunji for the first time. We went to a Haramatikk show and sat next to each other at the afterparty where the band mingled with their fans. At some point, I realized I didn't give a damn about Haramatikk anymore. I was more interested in Shunji himself.

Back at his apartment, I naturally went straight over to inspect his CD collection. It started with Aphex Twin and ended at Underworld. "I've never really been into metal," he confessed with a laugh, and his eyes were bright with a steady calm desperation that I completely misinterpreted.

If only I'd met him just a few weeks earlier. That night, I was shocked to learn he was only twenty-six, the same age as me; he looked much older. And that was before that whole chunk of hair at the front of his head turned white. None of this stopped me from moving in with him. "The only thing we have to fear," I said, "is fear itself." We believed in the salvific power of love, but what did that amount to? More bumper-sticker profundity. Our own private Tiananmen Square.

"Can I make a request?" shouted a voice from the moiré of faces beyond the bar.

"If it's in the binders." To gesture, I had to look for the source of the voice. It was the guy from Shunji's funeral. He turned away to leaf through the big binders that listed the tracks in Murata-san's collection. I emptied ashtrays and watched the back of his head. The ashtrays were in the shape of hollow skulls, cast from metal like roleplaying figurines. I polished each one with a rag, working my fingernails into the fiddly grooves between the teeth. Obviously, he'd asked someone at the funeral where I worked. It was equally obvious that he'd never have come in here without an ulterior motive. In a canvas jacket and jeans, he looked like he should have been browsing for computer parts in Akihabara, not jostling with our Friday crowd. My curiosity flickered like a torch with a weak battery. I took orders for two Salty Dogs, mixed them, washed the cocktail shaker.

He came back to the bar, easing gingerly between the

regulars. "Give the request form to him," I said, indicating Murata-san. But he kept shoving it at me until I caught sight of the writing on it. Resting a fist on my cocked hip, I struggled through the sloppily handwritten Japanese.

What time do you get off work? I need to talk to you. It's about Shunji. I'll wait for you in front of the east exit. Areiya

I looked up with an unformed question on my lips. He was gone.

Grinding my teeth, I scrumpled the note into my pocket. *Areiya,* in katakana? An online pseudonym. How fucking lame. And yet, looked at from another angle, it was a bold touch. It challenged me to take him more seriously. I accepted a handful of CDs from Murata-san's extended paw and jammed them into their places on the long shelves behind the bar. Angra, Anthrax, Arch Enemy... I still hadn't found Shunji's MP3 player, so he must have taken it with him to work on Wednesday. I'd meant to ask Natsume whether the family had got it back, but I'd forgotten. Maybe he'd been listening to it when his foot slipped on that ladder in the rain. Squarepusher or Jeff Mills, bloop bleep-a-loop bleep all the way down. He never had come to share my passion for metal. Cannibal Corpse, Cathedral, Children Of Bodom... What if Areiya had a good reason for stalking me in this furtive way? It was easy to laugh, but he'd acted as if he actually was trying to be invisible. As if he was trying to hide in plain sight.

And: he might be a loser, but he undeniably had one thing going for him. He wasn't dead.

The more I thought about his pale face, waiting for it to snag some specific recollection, the more it grew on me, like an indestructible fungus that glows in the dark, a cockroach that stays alive even after you stomp its guts out, or a bubbling sump of garbage full of bacteria that will outlive the human race. *Life!* The old compulsion was back. I wanted to plunge my hands in, feel the warmth of fermentation, and squeeze my fists full of wriggling maggots. *What's your secret?* But I knew the secret now, of course, and it had turned out to be boringly obvious, like all the big ones. There's no special trick to staying alive. You just have to be lucky. And there's no special trick to *that*, either. The dead are all the same. The living are all different.

Three hours later, cleaning the bathroom after the last customers had left, I checked myself out in the dim red light. Beneath my bleach blonde pixie cut, I looked ten years older than I was, thanks to the virulent combination of heavy metal and Aokigahara. But my eyes were bright and glassy. Leaning closer to the mirror, I knocked over my mop. I caught it and resettled it against the sink. Small skeletons clung to the washstand, one hauling the other up. I rubbed my fingers over their realistically discolored bones. I was used to them, but every so often they reminded me of the skeletons we'd seen in Aokigahara, sprawled twenty metres from a backpack with empty bottles of pills in it, or collapsed beneath a frayed end of rope that hung from a tree. The seven of us, or eight or nine or fifteen, had converged on each grisly discovery in rage and excitement; they were the high points of our trips. Mostly, in the depths of the forest, the bones were clean, if gnawed and scattered. But on two occasions, we'd found bodies within sight of the trails, and one of those couldn't have been dead for more than twenty-four hours. He'd looked alive until we got close enough to see where the wild dogs had torn at his dangling shin. I cried that time, and Egg puked. Aokigahara stripped people of their dignity, and that included us. But we kept at it for a total of nine expeditions, winter and summer and spring and fall, because we had a mission: "All this will be justified," Shunji said, "if we can save even one life."

Holding my breath, I leaned even closer to the mirror. The ornate silver cross that I wore around my neck swung forward, clinking on the taps. *There they were,* deep in my pupils: faint white brachiate shapes. I closed one eye. Then the other. Opened both eyes. Still there. I whirled away from the mirror, swallowing.

"Still raining," Murata-san said. "Need a ride?" He lived in Shibuya; I lived in Yoyogi, which was on his way. We stood in the grimy tiled forecourt above Axez, looking out at the downpour, and the silence felt like a song request form that Murata-san was waiting for me to fill in.

But if I gave him a title for my problem, I'd have to give him the whole song, and this was a song that could go on for hours if I let in, deteriorating into a grinding solo of pure noise. *My boyfriend is dead. He never really believed in love but he thought it might keep him safe and it never even occurred to him that he would be dragging me down with him. He did these calculations to figure out how long it would be until the next one of us died, and he was only one day off, and it was him. Now I'm the only one left, and according to the formula, I have three to twenty-five days to live. But I'm different. So I'm not really worried. Because I'm different. I'M JUST NOT SURE I'M DIFFERENT ENOUGH and I need information. Shunji before he died became like the world expert on Aokigahara Jukai but he said that 99% of the available information is bullshit, because the people who know aren't talking and the people who're talking don't know. Just like the suzuran tapes. Clitter shshh sshhrr. One dead end after another. And it's a million to one this Areiya is just some fucking otaku who heard about us on 2 channel before they shut those boards down —*

I shook my head. "Thanks, but I've got plans."

Murata-san nodded. "Take care then."

"Here's my problem," I said. "I don't know who you are. I apologize, but you're going to have to remind me where we met."

The stylized flowers in the stained glass panel behind Areiya wavered; the air itself seemed to wobble. When the ringing in my ears started to drown out the ambient noise of the pub, I realized I was holding my breath.

Areiya looked embarrassed. "Well, we've never met in person. But I knew Shunji. I really admire that kind of concern about social issues. I can't say we knew each other well, though. I only met him once —"

"When?"

"Wow." Areiya had to think about it. "Must have been

five years ago."

"*Where?*"

"Jukai. I think it was November."

"October," I whispered.

The legendary first expedition, when fifteen or sixteen posters on the Other Topics board had headed out to Yamanashi prefecture for the inaugural activity of the Jukai Volunteer Patrol Society, aka JuKyo. Only a few of them had ever met in person before, and more than half of them dropped out after that day. Even Shunji couldn't name everyone in the photographs they took in front of the Shuketsu trail marker, with the cryptic little Buddhist charm at the foot of the post, on the edge of the forest. There was Kott-san mugging with a plastic bag over his head, there was Egg pretending to strangle Maedaza – and there, too, must have been Areiya, one of the nameless ones standing in the back, his face disguised by the shadows of the pines that crouched behind the trail marker.

"I guess it could have been October. But I remember it was starting to get cold. We kept the campfire going all night. No one slept, and when we had to gather more firewood, we went in groups, tied together by a rope. I guess we should have just put up our tents. But it felt safer to stay awake... I mean, the *bones*. We found them when we were clearing our campsite. They were all heaped up in the only place where you could build a fire. We moved them, but you know. And then that shitty thing that happened to Wakabayashi-san..."

Ninnik. I still thought of them all by their pseudonyms – it was a way of keeping them alive in my mind, the way they'd lived on Shunji's and my computer screens for the last years and months and weeks of their lives (we used to check in with each other by IM, even after we got too scared to meet anymore). Only after he fell in front of the 7:52 out of Mitaka had Ninnik reverted to being plain old Teruo Wakabayashi.

"...you know? He fell into that hole."

Four metres deep, Ninnik himself had said, although

Shunji had said it was more like two.

"Yeah," I said. "In the dark. And when they shone the flashlight down, there were two bodies down there with him."

"And they were moving."

"Uh huh. He just made that up to scare the rest of you. And you fell for it,."

Areiya tilted his chin from side to side. He recrossed his legs so that one narrow denim knee poked high above the other. Rather than admit he'd been fooled, he would hype up the story, I predicted.

"They were at the worst stage." His dangling sneaker jiggled. "They'd started to... b-b-be eaten, so their faces were more skull than skin. But they were still dressed, and the woman's long hair was still in a clip. When we shone the light down, she was kind of sprawled with her head towards Wakabayashi-san. But the man was lying on his back and there was this kind of sh-sh-shadow on his t-shirt, where the weather hadn't faded it. You could see that she'd died with her head on his chest. She'd rested it there for months. *But then she'd moved.*"

I set my face hard.

"And Wakabayashi-san, he said that before we brought the flashlight up, he'd *heard* her coming for him." Areiya checked my expression, then laughed loudly. "He wasn't making it up. His eyes were bugged out like... When we hauled him out of there, he *ran* all the way back to the fire before he realized his ankle was fucked. And next day it was swollen up so badly we had to carry him back to the bus stop. On the stretcher that we'd brought for bodies! It was hell over that rough ground. We took the bones, though. We put them in a garbage bag—"

"Foxes," I said. "Or badgers." And then, before he could argue anymore, "Yeah, but isn't it crazy how the ground rises and falls? It's enough to make you seasick. And the roots everywhere. Really easy to trip."

"Yeah!" He nodded vigorously.

"That's why we ended up relying on the suzuran tape. Especially in winter. It stands out against the snow..." Abruptly, I shuddered. My mind's eye had inadvertently conjured the memory of those pink, yellow, orange, and blue ribbons, stretched and flapping between the bare trunks. Polyethylene rope, generically known as suzuran tape. Lily-of-the-valley tape, sold in rolls of 500 and 1000 meters. The further into the forest you went, the more of it appeared, strung from tree to tree in zigzag trails. In some places it was gathered into skeins. When the wind gusted through the forest, and the treetops soughed, you could hear it *slissing* and *clittering*.

"I remember," Areiya said. "They'd thought of everything, but they hadn't thought of that. So they made plans to bring some of their own next time."

"They did. We did." There was a tumbler on the table in front of me. I picked it up and drank. Neat whiskey. Areiya took a sip from his own glass. I said, "The trouble is that you can get mixed up. What's *your* tape and what's somebody else's. The fucking stuff is non-biodegradable; it doesn't even lose its color over time. And that was the real problem. You know you should be focused on the forest itself, but the trees all look the same, everything is green, and your eyes just naturally pick out the tape... those nice bright colors. So a lot of the time, we were following somebody else's trail. Accidentally or on purpose." I took another sizable gulp of whiskey. "And a lot of the time, we found them."

"I'm surprised you stuck it out," Areiya said. "I mean, there weren't any girls the time I went."

I shrugged. "Shunji did try to get me to quit."

Areiya put a match to one of his Marlboro Lights. When he had it going, he held it out to me. I shook my head. Why did he think I'd want a cigarette his mouth had touched? He drew back and sat smoking it himself, his face pinched and lonely. I rested my elbows on the table and watched droplets fly off the umbrellas of people coming into the bar. The bottoms of my jeans were still wet, too. In Japan, it starts raining around the end of May and doesn't let up until midsummer. I used to tell Shunji that I might end up leaving the country just to cure my MAD – Monsoon Affective Disorder. The mild form of this condition causes a desire to stay in bed all day listening to Nine Inch Nails's "Hurt" over and over again. A severely afflicted patient may find herself putting on a bold front to her few remaining friends, and then landing in a ghastly Irishesque bar at three in the morning to reminisce about her newly dead boyfriend with a stranger. And blaming everything on the fucking *rain*.

"I remember one time we found this cave," I said. "It was still daylight, so we played scissors-paper-stone and went in. Shunji took the lead. It was so narrow we had to go in single file, and so low we had to stoop. The roof was dripping cold water. It was March, maybe April. I was third back, behind Kott-san. Suddenly, I heard Shunji shout, and Kott-san slammed into me, trying to get the hell out of there. He always was a bit of a coward at heart. But I shoved him back and I caught up with Shunji. The tunnel had opened out. It was a *cavern* down there. The roof was thick with icicles as long as your arm. They glittered in the light from our torches... It was so beautiful. And I looked at Shunji and he had this, this *look* on his face. As if this was what he'd been searching for all his life —"

"The forest is riddled with caves," Areiya said, nodding. "It's all due to the topology of the area. When Mount Fuji erupted in the ninth century, several billion tons of magma flowed down from the number two crater, covering the foothills all the way to Lake Yamanashi." He spewed out the information, the useless information that was all you could ever find on the internet. "The irregularities of the land created air pockets in the lava as it cooled. Most of Jukai stands on about a foot of decomposed organic matter – you can't really call it soil. An extremely fragile ecosystem. And now Japan's largest remaining first-growth forest. They say there are monks living in there, holy men who live on mist and sunlight..."

94

"No one *lives* there," I snapped. "That's just a myth. Like: compasses don't work; packs of wild dogs roam the forest... We never met another living soul."

"But they did when I was with them. Just one."

"Huh? Oh, you mean that guy who seemed to be thinking about suicide."

I'd forgotten about that. They'd spotted him when they got off the train from Tokyo, a young man by himself, and nudged each other excitedly. They didn't see him on the bus, but half an hour down the trail that led into the forest, they'd come on him again. Standing with his hands in his pockets, quietly looking up at the trees. The hair had risen on the back of Shunji's neck. He went forward alone, tripping over tangled roots, and said, *You're not thinking about doing anything stupid, are you?*

The young man had angrily told Shunji to leave him alone. There was nothing more Shunji could really say after that, so he just slouched back to the others, and they never saw the guy again.

"There aren't any ghosts, either," I said. "Although I know the Japanese believe there are. Where would you be without your spooks and revenants?"

"Where would we be without a designated national suicide spot?" He almost smiled.

Tightly, I said, "I never did understand the logic that makes people go all the way to Jukai to kill themselves. I mean, you're still going to be alone when you die."

"They wouldn't be suicidal if they weren't pretty much alone to begin with. Would they? But maybe it makes them feel a little better at the end... maybe they don't feel so very alone. With all those spooks and revenants for company."

I'd been staring into my whiskey, but this brought my head up sharply. Areiya's crooked smile broadened. I suddenly saw how he would have fitted into JuKyo.

And that brought me back to the only questions that mattered.

Why had he never gone back after the first expedition?

What had he seen or suspected that all my friends had missed? And *why* (as a result?) *why was he still alive,* when they were dead?

I swallowed my desperation. If I lowered my guard, I might inadvertently give away whatever it was that he wanted from *me,* and then I'd be out of bargaining chips. I had no illusion that he might share his secret for free. When the Donner party were reduced to two survivors, do you think they split their rations? I think they fought over the last grisly scrap of flesh.

This conjecture, however, reminded me of the hikers whose bodies Ninnik had literally stumbled on top of. Everyone's account agreed on one point: they'd died in each other's arms. At first, the guys had taken it for a double suicide. But the discovery of their rucksacks, replete with provisions and possessions that included several forms of ID, cast doubt on that scenario. Suicides usually discarded their ID before they entered the forest – an unexpected spanner in the works of our mission: we'd originally planned to collect the personal effects of the suicides we found and deliver them to their families, so that they could find some peace. As it turned out, crushingly for Shunji, we were only able to do that in about a dozen cases. And most of those had appeared to be explorers like ourselves, who'd never intended to die, who'd just lost their way – or fallen into one of those pits – not fifty metres from the trail— "They should have been able to climb out!" I said aloud. "The pit wasn't *that* fucking deep. *Why didn't they climb out?*"

Areiya pushed his index fingers together in front of his mouth. His nails were dirty and ragged. After a moment he said, "I didn't go down in the pit, so I didn't see properly. But I think the man had broken his leg. It was kind of bent up. So he wouldn't have been able to move. And his girlfriend wouldn't leave him to get help." On the last words he looked me in the eye.

"Or maybe she was too scared," I said steadily.

"Maybe. Or maybe it was already dark when they fell into the pit. And before they could climb out, *something* found them."

I slammed back the dregs of my whiskey and pushed my chair away from the table. Too late, I saw Areiya's tiny smile and realized that he thought he'd scored.

In JuKyo, the guys had competed constantly to creep each other out. I'd stood aloof, like Shunji, but for different reasons; while he was simply unflappable – or so he fooled everyone into thinking – I had the protection of linguistic and cultural barriers. I was *American,* for God's sake. Dead bodies might gross me out, but ghosts and bogeymen? Give me a break. Well, that was then, this was now... but at Areiya's clumsy attempt to spook me, something of my old indignation had genuinely returned. My life was at stake here, and we were going to talk about nameless *somethings?* What the hell use was that?

I shoved my chair under the table and grabbed my bag. Areiya looked up at me. The skin around his eyes was translucent, cleaner than any other part of him. He said in a strenuously artificial tone, "Do you like movies? I'm kind of a movie buff, but there's this war movie, *Bataan,* made in the fifties – have you seen it? Anyway, that's what that pit reminded me of. The hero – he's a downed fighter pilot – is struggling through the jungle, and he falls into a pit that's disguised so it looks like part of the path... but it's not a real pit. It's a trap."

I had hold of myself now, and I said with scorn as light as air, "I haven't seen the movie, but I would guess the trap is symbolic. People build traps for themselves inside their own minds. Myths. Fear. Jukai." I gestured around the bar. "This city."

"You're pretty positive, aren't you," Areiya said, getting up.

"It's the American religion." I hesitated. "There are pool tables upstairs."

"Pool?"

He was barely on nodding terms with the world of English. "Oh God," I said. *"Billiards.* Come on, I'll kick your ass."

I sank another ball, followed up with an attempted bank shot, and missed. Ponderous hip-hop beats shivered the shadows like distant waves rolling over the surface of the city. Yet the room seemed to be filled with a hush that separated us from the other players, and the cone of light over our table enhanced my sense of isolation. Areiya paced around the table, squinting at the balls. I could see how badly he wanted to win, or at least hold his own. Tough; I wasn't going to let him.

I chalked my cue, thinking about the moment on Wednesday night when my life had changed. Natsume crying on the phone, the rain plipping outside. When I got off the phone, I'd whirled through our one-and-a-half rooms in a frenzy, emptying them of Shunji's clothes and books and all his CDs. I'd crammed everything into trash bags and hauled it down to the collection point. As if he'd dumped me, not died on me.

As if I thought his stuff was contaminated.

"So, can I ask," Areiya said. "Why did you come to Japan?"

"I was working retail in San Francisco," I said. "Felt like a change of scenery."

And last night when I got home there'd been a line of wet footprints on the concrete floor of the hall, leading almost to our door, or possibly to the neighbors'. Nothing unusual there. After all, it was raining. But as I dug for my keys, I'd smelled a sudden whiff of – *something*. Damp earth. Wet leaves rotting in a puddle. I broke two nails getting in that door. And later, when I lay down to try to sleep, my eyes started to feel funny. They *throbbed.* It didn't exactly hurt, but if I tried to keep them shut, I got the feeling that I was going to explode. I went into the bathroom. Beneath my swollen eyelids, I saw the same sludgy hazel orbs I'd known forever. The fluorescent light over the sink shrank my pupils to dots. But when I looked closer, I saw that their black was adulterated by silvery threads, like cobwebs. Or the roots of some plant that was growing deep in my eyes, reaching towards the surface.

What I did was I smashed the mirror. I used our frying-pan, and afterwards I swept up the pieces and threw them out.

I didn't want to remember how I'd felt while I was doing it. Instead, I watched Areiya speaking to me. He was asking dumb questions like a regular guy. I said, "One sister. No. Yeah," and I imagined his pale geeky body outspread in the mirrored ceiling of a love hotel, glistening like milk spilled in a depression. It seemed as if it should be possible to root out his secret from his body, squeeze it from the soft undersides of his biceps, suck it from the sensitive pelted tops of his thighs...

We were playing eight-ball, and I was solids. I took a safety shot.

"And what are you going to do now?" Areiya said, studying the impossible position I'd left him.

I shrugged. "Go back to America, I guess."

"California?"

"Yeah."

"Your family will be happy to see you."

I laughed. "It'll be like I've come back from the dead."

Areiya lit a cigarette. He hunched his shoulders and slouched over to the free-standing chrome ashtray. "Do you think California is far enough?"

"What do you mean?"

"Do you think you'll be safe there?"

"No one's safe anywhere. If you've been reading the boards online, you'll know..." At the end of this sentence I had to gasp for air, but Areiya didn't react. With his pale pointed impassive face and the unwashed black hair that swept across it, the smoke from his cigarette curlicuing up around him, he looked as if he would never react to anything. I *wanted* what he had, and I was getting more and more impatient with this game.

"Shunji and I were going to move to the States someday," I said. "Only that got put on hold when he landed the job at Takada. It was his first – you have to understand how important it was to him. The idea that he might be able to fit into this society, after all. Because he never had been able to... It's not that he was a misfit. He used to organize DJ events and art shows; he always had that talent for getting people into action. And he always wanted... he was always *giving*. He was just a naturally good person—"

"Why did he start JuKyo?"

Why? WHY? How about more than 40,000 suicides in this country every year? "Well, it was after the police cancelled their annual sweep. I think it was in the news, so they were chatting about it online. The budget cuts, the public perception that taxpayers' money was being wasted... and so Shunji said, why don't we take over. No publicity, just—"

"If he didn't want publicity, 2 Channel was the wrong place to discuss it," Areiya said.

"That wasn't him. It wasn't any of us."

I knew what he was talking about: at one point during JuKyo's active period, a rival crew of spookophiles over on 2 Channel had found out about us and expended a lot of energy dissing us online. A couple of years after that, some of them decided to copy us. They even wrote a book about their expeditions. By that time, JuKyo was already defunct and Bu-Taro and Maedaza were already dead, with Egg to follow (a lethal dose of gin on top of sleeping pills, 699 days ago) before the book was published. So maybe it was out of tact or shame that the 2 Channel crew never breathed a word about us in public. And maybe it was out of tact or shame that the 2 Channel administrators deleted every board and every thread in which JuKyo had been discussed. But that, of course, only intensified the fascination among those who already knew our story – and those who arrived later, to prowl around the internet and pick up details of each subsequent tragedy, like wild dogs circling a campfire.

"We didn't want to glamorize the place! We were for real.

I'm saying – we were for real. OK, so it started out as a joke. But then Shunji got the rest of us thinking. Like, shit, maybe I *can* do something to help other people."

Areiya bounced off the wall. "So completely stupid," he said, voice thick – the first time I'd seen any genuine emotion from him. *"None* of them were thinking about helping other people. They were only in it for themselves. Some of them wanted to see ghosts. Some of them wanted to see corpses. Some of them were just along for the ride. Hey, it's a free country! Knock yourselves out. Nail your stupid little boxes of flyers to the trees. But don't talk about *helping* people!"

My hostility evaporated in a flash. It dawned on me that Areiya must have been sincere about the JuKyo mission. When the others started fooling around, telling crude jokes and ghost stories, talking loudly about music, he must have felt betrayed and angry. Alone among them. Except for...

"That's how Shunji felt, too," I said. "He used to agonize about it. He *knew* half of them were there for the chills and the other half were just along for the ride. But in the end, he figured it didn't matter if they could get the job done. If they could *save* people..."

"No one can be saved." Areiya's voice was almost inaudible. "Everyone's going to die."

For an instant I wanted to run screaming. Instead, I shuffled around into his field of vision. "Hey, you know, it doesn't help to think about it."

"Not think about it? And how do you do that, exactly?"

"I mean, if you just focus on what you can do in the present – "

"That's my point. It was never about other people. They were just gratifying their own psychological needs." Areiya's lips shook. He'd probably been saying these things to Shunji inside his head for years, I realized. Now he had to make do with me. "The sheer *selfishness* of these people who go looking for thrills under the *pretense* of volunteer work – "

"Shunji had a younger brother," I said. I was betraying a secret, but what did it matter now? "Hirotaka. He committed suicide when he was eighteen. In Jukai. At least, that's what his note said. So maybe you're right: Shunji had a selfish motivation. He never did find Hirotaka's body, by the way. Does that devalue what – what we *achieved?* We got emails from people who found our flyers…"

I trailed off because Areiya's face betrayed a reaction even more marked than I'd hoped for. He didn't merely look dismayed. He looked stricken. "I didn't know." His adam's apple jumped. He regarded the cigarette in his fingers as if he didn't know how it had got there. "So they've only got one child left now. Two suicides in a single family!"

"Shunji did *not* kill himself," I said mechanically.

Areiya seemed to master himself. At last he said, "Why are you so sure of that?"

I closed my eyes. They throbbed.

"I mean. If he didn't… what's the alternative?"

"That's what I hoped you were going to tell me," I said to the darkness.

I heard the clunk of pool balls and opened my eyes. Areiya had plonked the triangle on the table. He was gathering our unfinished game into it. "I've got a theory, actually. But before I say anything, I need to take a look at that rooftop."

Scuttling across Shinjuku in the rain, I foresaw a kind of negative satisfaction that I knew well. We'd be unable to glean a damn thing from this adventure. It would be just like when the six of us had gone to check out Sumidabashi, the bridge off of which Bu-taro had allegedly jumped. We'd stood there in the cold wind and understood that we would never know *why* he'd died… and that had been strangely reassuring. Egg in his woolly tassel hat, Kott-san with his atopic dermatitis and glasses, Ninnik who was a mine of movie trivia, Maedaza in the leather jacket he would be wearing 379 days later when he knotted his motorbike around an el support, and Shunji with his arm around me… we'd stood there in a silence that was less elegiac than it was dimly complacent. Far below, excursion boats wriggled through the grey waves like amphibious larvae. The traffic thudded across the bridge, and we stood there like a line of trees.

"He was so-utsubyo," Ninnik had said at last, and Shunji murmured the translation to me: "Manic-depressive." I hadn't known that, and relief burst in my chest like a floppy cotton firework.

"Yeah. Talk about high risk," Egg said, making a show of eyeballing the distance down to the water. Then we all laughed.

But when Shunji and I got home, we put on *Jigoku Dayori*, the Haramatikk album that Bu-taro had liked best, and hit repeat on his favorite track. "I am ask, why is this place too cold." We held each other, swaying in the choppy beat. "Never know you beside me, never find love." I cried a little then, luxuriously.

We'd all learned our lines from music. That was what had brought us together. As it turned out, that expedition to Sumidabashi would be the end of JuKyo; subsequently we only met at funerals. But from that day to this, when the going got tough, it was music that I turned to, and I knew the others had done the same.

I shot a glance at Areiya from underneath the dripping edge of my vinyl umbrella. He had an umbrella of his own – blue with rusted ribs, one of them broken – but he carried no messenger bag or rucksack. And now I noticed something else: unusually for someone of our generation, he had no earphone cord looped from his pocket or dangling around his neck.

I fingered the MP3 player in my own pocket. Four gigabytes of hard rock and metal, the homeopathic antidote to this city. If Areiya hadn't been with me, I would automatically have had the thing on now.

Like many of the older buildings in West Shinjuku, the building where Shunji had worked was a microcosm of the city itself: a cell phone shop and a designer thrift store on the ground floor, an Italian restaurant on the second floor, a consumer credit agency on the third floor, and offices the rest of the way up. The Tokyo branch of Takada Industries, Ltd. had the eighth through tenth floors. I would have liked to see Shunji's desk and poke through his drawers, if they hadn't been cleaned out already, but there was no way past the automated card locks. So we kept climbing the emergency stairs, and arrived breathless on the topmost landing, behind a metal door that looked both heavy and locked, but opened easily to a push from Areiya's fingertips. I half expected a siren to go off. Instead, we emerged from the penthouse to the soft roar of rain and distant traffic.

Areiya paced around the perimeter of the roof. About the size of a tennis court, it had only one feature, apart from the penthouse: a cylindrical water tank on stilts. The concrete wall around the roof's edge rose as high as my waist and was topped in turn by a wire fence. I wondered how the hell Shunji had gotten over it. The flares of color from neon signs on neighboring rooftops seemed to slow Areiya's progress, like a strobe light. I made a circuit around the penthouse. Despite the rain, it was bright enough to see that the entire expanse of the roof was empty. I returned to the open doorway and waited until Areiya came back.

"What are you thinking?" he said.

He'd left his umbrella beside me; the rain flattened his hair and soaked the shoulders of his jacket.

"Did you find anything?" But I knew he hadn't. He squatted beside me, shaking out a cigarette. He offered me the pack, and this time I took one. "Your existence has screwed up my theory," I said after a couple of inhales."And your theory was?"

"That everyone who went on the *first* expedition was dead."

He smiled faintly, either ridiculing my suggestion or acknowledging its logic, I couldn't tell which. "Maybe my turn hasn't come yet."

"No, because Shunji – he was the leader. So it makes sense that he would be the last."

"That does make sense," Areiya admitted. "But then, why shouldn't it be everyone who ever – "

"The 2 Channel guys; nothing ever happened to them! And the hikers every summer – "

"Everyone who was in JuKyo."

"Shunji tried to stay in touch with them all, but some of them never wrote back. But I know they're still out there making trouble on the internet, so it's obviously not everyone who *ever* participated. But... I never met anyone else from the *first* expedition. They just vanished back to wherever they came from." No need to underline the fact that Areiya had done the same. And besides, he'd reappeared, while they hadn't, because – "I still think they're probably dead. And I figure... I think... I wonder..." It was almost impossible to say it out loud. "I wonder if something *happened* on that expedition. Something so bad that not even Shunji could ever bring himself to tell me about it."

Areiya ashed his cigarette between the toes of his sneakers. They were black Chuck Taylors, the rubber toes grey with age and smeared with mud – quite a feat when there was no bare earth in Shinjuku. "It was the worst experience of my life," he said in a curiously flat tone.

I held my breath.

"But what makes you different?" Suddenly, he turned to me. "Why should I – why should I accept this theory of yours?"

I could have given him a million reasons, but they all started with *Because I'm AMERICAN goddamn it and I only went with them in the first place because I was in love with Shunji and I DON'T WANT TO DIE –*

Down on the street it had been barely chill, the rain no colder than the air, but in climbing ten floors we seemed to have climbed two months backwards in the year. Clammy with cooled sweat, my shirt clung to my back under my lightweight leather jacket. Icicles in April. "If you've got a better theory," I muttered.

"I should have thought Shunji would have a theory." His voice held a strangulated hint of rage. He lifted his shoulders and made a face. I understood better than I would have liked to: after all, I was angry with Shunji, too.

"He had a theory for every day of the week," I said. "And none of them could ever be proved. Or disproved." The only thing Shunji had ever come up with that held was the formula, and that was simply a matter of crunching the easily observable fact that the intervals between our friends' deaths were getting shorter. If you started with Maedaza at day 379 since Bu-taro's death, the dates turned out to fit the series of prime numbers, skipping sixty, then forty-eight, thirty-six, etcetera. And that made it look like Kott-san, who was into applied mathematics. But then Kott-san died, too.

Unwilling to confess that we'd actually reached the point of suspecting our friends, I left that part out when I told Areiya about the formula.

"Prime numbers!" Unexpectedly, he laughed out loud. "No way!"

"With a margin of error in the neighborhood of two weeks," I said.

"Ah, well then. So when's your number up?"

He was smiling at me as if he thought it was all a big joke.

I stood up and went out into the rain. When I dragged on my cigarette, it had gone out – soaked instantly. Just as well, I guess, but why shouldn't I smoke? Why shouldn't I allow myself to get wet through? I walked to the edge of the roof, my head lighter than my body, and started around the perimeter as Areiya had done. I saw that there was a ledge about a meter down, above the windows of the floor where Shunji had worked. I kept my eyes on that. Below, the traffic on Koshu-kaido trailed past out of focus, a string of blurry red tears.

Areiya caught up with me. He brushed against my shoulder. Irritably, I sidestepped. "I'm looking for his MP3 player," I said, jabbing my finger at the fence. My voice clattered. "I never got it back. I wanted to find it."

"Why? I mean – sentimental value?"

"Why? *Why*? You tell me."

"I never loved anyone," he said after a minute. "I wouldn't know."

I stiffened and drew in my shoulders. We plodded on. I said, "You don't even have an MP3 player. Or a Discman or anything. Do you?"

His face showed confusion. "Why should I?"

"Oh, I don't know," I almost screamed. "Why do you keep forcing *me* to make the connections? What are you here for if you aren't going to help me out?" I caught myself. "Why don't you tell me your theory."

"No, but this is really interesting. About the iPod. Is it something to do with the series of prime numbers?"

"Then you do. It's not just me." My hand went into my pocket and I touched my own MP3 player in a rapture of horror, remembering how often since Shunji's death I'd reached for it out of sheer habit. Sorrow had saved me, making it seem like too much trouble to do something as simple as untangling the earphone cord.

"Do you think portable music players had something to do with their deaths?" Areiya's voice was frank, but his eyes held a sparkle.

"Not necessarily *portable –* " I stumbled over his formal descriptive term— "but it's the only common factor. At first I was focused on *why*. We all were. But to hell with *why*. Let the, the fucking ontological questions look after themselves. Let's look at *how*. And nobody else thought of this, it only occurred to me after I couldn't find his MP3 player, but *they were all listening to music when they died.* Hirai-san on his bike, which is so dangerous but he always did, Eguchi-san at home, Wakabayashi-san had his iPod on when he fell or jumped or was pushed in front of that train, Tanabe-san had the stereo on … and Shunji. I just *know* he had his MP3 player on. He came up here for a break, because he was working late again. To listen to music. Alone."

"You didn't mention Kikkawa-san," Areiya objected. "What about him?"

I shrugged impatiently. "Who knows? Maybe his MP3 player got lost in the river."

"Or maybe he really did commit suicide."

I felt a weight coming off my chest, similar to the way I'd felt on Sumidabashi when Ninnik said *You know, he was manic-depressive.* "Yeah. That's the other thing I was thinking. He doesn't fit into any formula because he up and killed himself before it... whatever it is... So you... you agree with me? The others..."

After an excruciating pause, Areiya slowly nodded. "They were... pushed." My relief didn't have time to flower before he continued, "But I still don't see where you're coming from with this theory." We'd made almost a full circuit of the roof. Just before we moved into the shadow of the water tank, I saw the indulgent smile on his face. He wasn't taking me seriously. "I mean, you were listening to that loud stuff today! At work! Why shouldn't that have done it?"

"Because I wasn't alone," I said, remembering how close I'd come to switching the stereo on at home last night. I would have had Testament or Pantera blasting through the apartment, if I hadn't been intent on listening for sounds from outside. "I think when they were alone, the music *changed...*"

"Into a subliminal command to commit suicide?"

"Yeah, why not?"

"You're hardly alone on a crowded Chuo line platform."

"You are if you've got an iPod on. That's the whole point."

"OK, well, leaving that aside. If you'd found Shunji's MP3 player—" Areiya gestured down at the ledge— "assuming he conveniently took it off, and the police didn't find it – what would you have done with it?"

I glanced around. The neon played relentlessly on the wet roof.

"Would you have *put it on?*"

I swallowed.

"Or would you have had *me* put it on?" His voice hardened; his smile softened the edges of his suspicion, like rot around the edges of cut fruit. I stumbled back against the fence. "Without saying a word about your theory, would you have handed it to me and said *hey, check out what he was listening to?*"

"Fuck you." I forced a laugh.

His face creased and crumpled. "I'm just kidding." He dashed both hands over his face as if to wipe away his laughter along with the rain that glossed his cheeks. "I mean – subliminal commands embedded in music! That's just – it's even wackier than forcefitting the dates into the series of prime numbers. You must have seen that movie, *Ringgu?* It even got a Hollywood remake. *The Ring.* I was expecting them to call it *The Video Cassette of Doom,* like a proper American horror movie." He giggled, reminding me what an otaku he was. "That was a cute plot device. But Lily? It was a *movie.*"

"You have to admit it makes sense, though," I argued. "It's the *only* common factor. And then I meet you, and you don't even have a fucking *Walkman.*"

"Why should I? I don't like music."

His face came into the brightest of the neon flares, the red glow from the Aiful sign, and his teeth shone in his smile, except for the left front one, which was bad. Funny I hadn't noticed that before.

But there were a lot of things I hadn't noticed before.

Music was my passion. It had been the same for all the guys in JuKyo. And sure, it was a common factor, and I'd felt a perverse satisfaction in contemplating the notion that the thing we loved best had turned against us with a lethal vengeance, or had turned out to be our collective weak point. But I might as well have said the common factor was that they'd all been *breathing.*

Music was my passion, and I tended to assume that it

occupied a more or less exalted place in other people's lives, too. Sloppy of me, admittedly, but given the kind of crowd I hung out with, I was seldom wrong in practise.

Yet Areiya had obviously been ill at ease in Axez. When he came in, Haramatikk had been playing. That would have been a good excuse to start a conversation, and he hadn't used it. Hadn't said anything, then or later, to make me think that he even knew who Haramatikk were.

But even that wasn't enough to trigger the numb neurons in my brain. I had to have it spelled out for me.

I don't like music.

So what were the chances that Areiya would have been looking at the Haramatikk website six years ago?

And to clinch it, he'd said *If they didn't want publicity they shouldn't have discussed it on 2 Channel,* and I should have understood right there that he thought we'd all come together on 2 Channel in the first place.

He hadn't known about Jukyo until 2 Channel outed us.

So how could he have been on the first expedition? How could he have described it in such flawless detail?

My stomach knotted. I licked rain off my upper lip.

The penthouse had two storeys. An iron staircase zigzagged up one of its sides to a closed door. Areiya was between me and the emergency stairs, so I went for the penthouse staircase, calling over my shoulder as I moved at an easy lope, "I want to check; maybe he left it up there."

As I climbed, Areiya's footfalls shook the stairs behind me. The door to the second storey, which must have been used for storage, didn't open when I turned the knob; but there was a ladder that led up from the small landing where I stood. I spidered up, gripping the verticals, hand over hand. I didn't trust the narrow iron treads, which were rusty as well as slick with rain. A forest of satellite dishes and antennae sprouted from the flat roof of the penthouse. I pushed up from one knee and stood erect among them.

Areiya's face appeared over the edge of the roof, set and

livid.

I moved away to peer between the satellite dishes in a pretense of looking for Shunji's MP3 player. The rain battered the exposed nape of my neck.

"This is where he fell from." Areiya had his back to me. He was gazing down at the alley behind the building. Even on Friday night, come four thirty in the morning, Shinjuku empties out. Unplugged electric signs, motorbikes in silver tarp coats, garbage bags piled for collection – it all looked a lot further down from up here. "He wouldn't even have had to jump outward to clear the fence."

I regarded the pale slimy side of his face. "I thought you said he was pushed."

"It's a fine distinction."

"And you're not much of a one for fine distinctions, are you? Such as the distinction between the truth and a lie."

Instead of speaking, I could have simply pushed him. But God help me, I couldn't commit murder on the basis of my own paranoia and a string of coincidences – such as that he'd known the way to this building, and how to get in after business hours…

"So you've worked it out." His shoulders seemed to slump as if a degree of tension had departed from him. "I've worked out that you've been lying to me. Because you've got something to hide." And what a technique I had for encouraging him to reveal it. I dug my fingernails into my elbows.

"Haven't lied to you. Not once. You just assumed." Still with his back turned to me, he placed one hand on the edge of the satellite dish beside him. Steadying himself. Or just plain holding on. And that looked a whole lot like he didn't trust me, either. Could he read my *mind?*

"My bad," I said. "I assumed you were part of the first JuKyo expedition. Because you *said* – " And I stopped, because it now dawned on me that he was right. I *had* assumed. He *hadn't* said. Not in as many words. Oh, this fucking language.

Japanese isn't big on pronouns. You can have a whole

conversation without them. So I'd just gone ahead, like I always did, and filled them in for myself. *He, him...* when I should have been filling in *I, me.*

"You were the guy they met in the forest," I breathed. "Oh, Areiya."

My heartbroken tone didn't seem to get through to him. "I was," he said tonelessly.

"So talk to me. Tell me..." I still wanted to hear how he'd survived.

"I didn't want to die." He shivered, shifting his weight, and adjusted his grasp on the rim of the satellite dish. His fingers probed across the bare plastic surface as if seeking a better grip. "I changed my mind. I don't want to die, I said. But they – he said it was too late. Too late? Everything I ever did was *too late.* I was in debt, my mother racked up more debts, she lent money to that boyfriend of hers and the asshole just gambled it away, and it was all in my name. I couldn't make my college loan payments. And there's that fucking forty-inch TV staring at me every time I come home, and the DVD recorder, she bought the shit on layaway, so I can't even sell it on the sly... but what does any of that matter? *None* of it matters. I saw that as clear as day, as soon as I lost it all. But he wouldn't change his mind. Too late, he said. It's too late for you, Areiya. And then I couldn't go back."

His monologue ended on a harsh note that threatened to segue out of control. The satellite dish rocked on its base. I clamped my lips on a scream.

"So your name really is Areiya," I said. It was the light. It had to be the light. His fingers writhed restlessly over the rim of the satellite dish, like blind roots seeking a light of their own. They seemed to be *stretching.*

He choked out a laugh. "My mother's bright idea." I'd forgotten what I asked him until he continued, "*A* for *Asia, rei* for *quiet, ya* for *arrow.* Only flash of creativity she ever has, and she gives me a name no one can read, so on the first day of school, there's every kid staring at me."

Oh God, his fingers were twice as long as they should

have been. Their probing nails almost reached the center of the satellite dish.

"And that's all it takes for the bullies to pick on you." Another shiver. "But none of that matters now. It's all gone, and I'd do anything to get it back. I'd give anything to... to see my mother again."

"Who..." Independently of my conscious will, my entire body was attempting to move backwards, away from those impossibly long fingers that seemed to be growing before my eyes like bamboo shoots in the rain. But I could feel the ribby frame of an aerial against my shoulders and I didn't want to knock it over and make a noise. "Who are *they*? Who's *he*? Who's the one who said you couldn't... couldn't go back anymore? Not *Shunji?*"

"Oh, no." He laughed, his shoulders shaking. I realized that more than anything in the world, I wanted him not to turn around. "Shunji was the one who could have saved me. It wasn't too late then. When they found me there was still time. It would have been a near thing – *he* already had his hooks into me – but they still could have saved me. *But they didn't.*"

I said in a cold voice, "Well, what made you their responsibility? Why should they have saved you? And why did they have to die because they didn't?"

He shook his head. I glimpsed his profile in silhouette against the neon. His eyelashes and eyebrows flew in sharply defined halos. Surely his cheekbones hadn't been that sharp, nor the hollows beneath them that pronounced— "I wouldn't have hurt them. A bunch of city kids decked out with the latest technology, causing trouble for regular people... that's just how it is. So I argued with him. Can you believe that. I'm completely in his power, and I'm *arguing* with him. I said, why do they have to die, they had good intentions ... and he said, *Because. Because I say so. I'm yours now and you are mine. All of them must die.*" His voice wavered rapidly between a low growl and a falsetto shriek. Then it returned to something like human. "But it took me ages to track them down, and by the time I did, one of them was already gone. So how'm I supposed to make up for that." As he spoke, his fingers moved convulsively. Their tips writhed backwards, bending the wrong way from the knuckles, seeking me, as if they had eyes. My stomach went loose and watery. I involuntarily took that step away from him. The aerial scraped past my arm and twanged back.

"I wasn't there," I said. I was whining for mercy. "I had nothing to do with it!"

"You were already in his life. He was trying to impress you in his mind. You were a part of him. The same way *he's* a part of me." Suddenly, Areiya snapped his hand back to his chest. He hunched over, hugging himself. His fingers snaked around his shoulders from both sides. They spread across his back like a diabolical external set of ribs. "I'm giving you a chance. You *had* a chance. You still— Run!" he screamed, full-throated. "Run! *Run!*"

But all I heard was the promise of brutality in his voice and all I saw were those boneless fingers wrapping around his back, his own body enslaving him to itself, and I gave myself over to an answering instinct as uncontestable as the urge to step on a poisonous spider. I took a swift step forward. My hands rose towards his back.

He wailed again and spun around, opening his arms. The horrifically long fingers darted out and fastened on my elbows, forcing my hands into the air. They weren't boneless but they had too many joints. Blackish-green spots stained their slimy skin like the markings of a frog. They writhed down my sleeves as if seeking a way through my jacket. Yet I barely tried to fight them because Areiya's face had changed so dramatically that my brain froze like an overloaded computer, unable to process – the skin stretched over the bones, so saturated with rain that it was coming apart, like the skin on some of the things I'd seen in Jukai, the things that were dead; the nostrils gaping straight at me. Worst of all were the eyes, or rather the hollows where they'd been. Out of their sockets, clusters of white tentacles or roots or malformed appendages writhed and tested the rain, some of them mere filaments and others as thick as my little finger. These growths had burst out from between Areiya's eyelids, stretching them agonizingly wide, although in his left eye, amid the filaments, a glimmer of anguished black remained.

They were the same things I'd seen in my own eyes.

Fully grown. Or getting there.

My mouth stretched open. I tried to scream.

"Acknowledge your master," the growling whine of a voice said, using Areiya's mouth, whose lips had thinned and cracked. Blood as dark as mud spilled down his chin when he spoke. *"Bow before the omnipotent illustrious ME I HIM IT WE,"* it licked bloody lips, *"what is mine ALL MINE – "*

My scream reached the air.

"None of that! It's too late." With this angry imprecation, one hand left my shoulder and darted at my face.

The fingers plunged into my mouth.

Down my throat.

They filled my mouth and worked deeper. I gagged on the taste of mouldering leaves. Unable to breathe, I succumbed to sheer panic.

I shook my head like a dog and *bit.*

Bones cracked. The taste of rotten meat flooded my mouth. My gag reflex went into hyperdrive. Scrabbling inside my mouth, fending off Areiya's other hand with my free arm, I dragged his severed fingers out of my throat. Retching, I flung them away.

He tore at my arms, one of his hands mutilated and trailing drops of that dark blood that I could still taste, both of them seeking my face. He wanted my mouth and eyes. ALL MINE.

We swayed on the edge of the penthouse roof. Satellite dishes toppled. I managed a short punch to his chest. Something cracked and my knuckles sank *into* his chest cavity, stretching the fabric of his shirt inwards, before I pulled back. He spat into my face. His phlegm smelled like vomit and burned my cheeks. But he spoke with Areiya's voice. "Try harder! Try your best!" His lips cracked at the corners; his mouth tore wider, expanding into a skull's grin. All his teeth but for the bases of a few molars were rotten and black.

I gave one more almighty push. His weight dropped out of my grasp. I collapsed.

On hands and knees on the edge of the penthouse roof, I saw to my despair that I hadn't pushed him far enough.

He twisted in the air. Instead of going over the wire fence, all the way to the street below, he hit the inside of the fence. He rebounded from it, fell to the rooftop, and lay still.

Moaning, I knelt on all fours and watched him fixedly.

For an eternal moment, he didn't move. Then I saw one of his arms twitch. With excruciating languor, it constructed itself into a brace to prop his upper body off the roof. The other arm hung shattered and limp.

Slowly, leaving behind a dark tracery that the rain immediately washed away, he dragged himself towards the emergency stairs.

Hunkering down and sidling around the penthouse roof, I followed his progress. To my horror, he seemed to regain strength as he moved. By the time he reached the doorway where we'd left our umbrellas, he was making good speed at a three-legged crawl.

I virtually flattened myself to the roof, praying that out of sight was out of mind.

But in front of the doorway, he rolled half onto his back. The obscenely torn corpse's smile faced upwards. The nests of roots curled in his eyesockets like fists with too many fingers. "You can't win," he shouted. His voice was impossibly strong. "You're all alone! You'll never beat *him!*"He flipped over like a fish submerging and flung himself into the stairway door.

I lay on my stomach in the rain. I didn't dare to take my eyes off the door for one second. I would watch it without blinking until dawn.

But a few minutes later, I gave in to the urge to search the roof for the fingers that I'd bitten off. I couldn't shake the fear that they might somehow reanimate themselves and come after me like snakes.

Near where we'd fought, I found them; or what was left of them. Whatever flesh they'd had, the rain had melted it. A few scraps of skin and fingernail clung to the bones, whose splintered ends reminded me suddenly of chicken bones.

I vomited. In a moment I retched up a lump that scraped my throat. Half crazed with disgust, I bent over again, urging my body on like a trainer exhorting a frothing horse. I wanted my stomach to be empty.

Finally, exhausted and depleted, I scanned the roof once more and then lay down on my back. I opened my mouth and let the acid Tokyo monsoon patter in.

"Breakfast," Murata-san said. He opened the fridge. Shaking his head at its lack of contents, or possibly at the ratty collection of postcards and DJ event flyers magneted to its door – most of them years old – he turned back to the draining board, where he'd put down a plastic bag from Quick Stop. He'd been holding it when I came out of the hospital with two stitches in my lower lip, a bubble pack of antibiotics in my pocket, and glossy smears of ointment on my face that made the marks of Areiya's spittle look like burn scars. The emergency room doctor had said: *Accident?* I could have assented, but I'd had enough of accidents that weren't. So I'd said, *Fight. I work in a bar...* And she'd nodded and got on with stitching me up.

I'd called Murata-san as soon as it was light. I'd known he would meet me in Shinjuku and take me to the hospital with no questions asked. I hadn't expected that he would drive me home afterwards – *still* asking no questions, so that if I wanted to stop him, I'd have had to throw his kindness back in his face. Which was more than I could do.

Truth be told, if not for him, I mightn't have come home at all. I might have gone straight to the airport.

Yet it felt strange to have him here. His gaze had roved coolly over the destroyed living-room, finding the all-too-obvious gaps where Shunji's things were missing. I'd opened my mouth to explain, then retreated to the bedroom to get out of my filthy, wet clothes.

Now, showered and dressed in a hoodie and a pair of sturdy jeans, I watched him sliding bread into the crumb-laden toaster oven. "Like your egg fried or boiled?"

"However you normally fix it... Murata-san? Uh..."

"Normally make do with a cup of coffee and a Marlboro. But I did know how to fix a mean omelette once upon a time."

"Omelettes," I said blankly, and then clapped my hands. I had a surreal feeling. "Omelettes."

There were some wrinkled green peppers in the vegetable drawer, and I found a lump of cheddar behind the only other thing in the fridge – half of a sixpack of Asahi, the last beer Shunji had ever drunk. The mouldy spots on the cheese reminded me of the markings on Areiya's skin. Bile surged in my throat. But the spots were easily shaved off."Shunji's gone," I said when Murata-san's attention was fully occupied with the frying pan and spatula.

"Figured."

"He's dead."

Murata-san dipped his head.

"What did you think?" I said. "That we had a fight and he walked out? No."

"What'd you do, then? Slip in the bath?"

The toaster oven pinged. Reprieved, I went to juggle the crusty slices onto plates.

We ate at the low table in the living-room. Outside, the rain had stopped. I took that as a good sign. Thousands of years of human history, after all, taught that the sun was on our side. Light bathed the room, the same color as the butter melting on my toast. I took tiny bites, hunger warring with the unpleasant pulling sensation in my lip where the anaesthetic was fast wearing off. "Cheese tastes fine," Murata-san said with his mouth full. "Come to think of it, they make aged cheeses. *Blue* cheese. Guess it doesn't matter if it turns." The sun caught his eyes, illuminating his translucent brown irises. His pupils were intelligent black dots. I felt sick at heart. My own eyes still weren't back to normal. I'd confirmed it in a mercilessly well-lit bathroom at the hospital. The silvery ghosts of roots might have shrunk and faded a little, but they were still there, and I knew what that meant.

If I'd got on the next plane for California, as I really wanted to, I'd have been signing my own death certificate.

Not to mention whoever Areiya would have fixated on next, once I was out of his reach. He might already have eliminated all the original members of JuKyo, but there remained their relatives... friends... Natsume... Murata-san himself... From my own experience, I knew that any mission that took on society itself was easier to start than to stop. One justification would flow naturally from the last. There was no logical stopping point.

"Everything OK?" said Murata-san, and I knew he wasn't talking about the food.

"Fine," I snapped.

Areiya had to *be* stopped. And soon.

That fall would have killed or mortally injured a human being... or anything that didn't have the power to regenerate itself as it moved. So what did I have to do? Blast his head off with a shotgun? Run him over with a bulldozer? Push him off fucking Rainbow Bridge – *no, that wouldn't work.*

Out of nowhere, my late grandmother spoke to me. A Russian immigrant, she used to spend hours a day before her Orthodox ikons. Her folk beliefs had contributed to my own perception of religion as a hopeless mixture of doctrine and superstition. *The devil loves to be where there is water.*

It was she who'd given me the silver cross I always wore.

Convulsively, I clutched it. I looked at it in the palm of my hand. I'd noted, but hadn't really *noticed,* that like Areiya's teeth, it had turned almost entirely black.

Oh. My. God.

I hiked up the hem of my hoodie and frantically polished the cross, almost unaware that Murata-san had stopped eating to watch me. To my relief, the black taint came off, leaving the silver clean – it wasn't some kind of acid, it was more like a coating of sticky tar. I relaxed my activity and met Murata-san's quizzical gaze.

"Yeah. Well," I said. "I met someone who turned out to be under some kind of…" I winced. "Don't believe me, OK, but I think he was dead."

Murata-san blinked. He looked down and speared his last piece of omelette with his fork, but didn't raise it to his lips. "That's pretty extreme. But… yeah. Last night. Kind of felt something hanging over you."

I shivered.

He hulked to his feet. "Coffee."

I listened tensely for clues that he was dialing someone to come and get me, but all I heard was the clink of the carafe and the gurgle of coffee being poured. He came back and set down steaming mugs. Then he lowered himself crosslegged to the tatami again.

"Dead, huh?"

I giggled, which was something I never did. "Rotting on his feet." With that, all of my disgust and panic returned, and I clamped my hands over my mouth, struggling to hold my breakfast down.

"Steady," Murata-san said. "Have tonight off if you like," he added. "Me and Kiyo-chan can handle it."

"Thanks. I was going to take the night off, anyway," I said, striving for the cheeky tone I often adopted with him.

"Got plans?"

"Not yet."

"Your zombie pal waiting for you?"

I sipped my coffee and eyed Murata-san across the table. It was unlike him to participate in someone else's elaborate joke, if that's what he took it for. He had a line in subtle allusive humor, but I couldn't see the creases at the corners of his eyes that usually passed for a smile. And his silence felt different from his normal monosyllabic manner. Like last night, he was waiting for me to put him in the frame. He wasn't going to invade my privacy or utter an opinion until I asked for it. Maybe this was sensitivity, or maybe it was just because he was my boss, but I resented his cool suspension of judgement, the implication that he was waiting for me to explain myself. Fuck that. I didn't have to explain myself to anyone.

"Go to hell," I muttered. Murata-san's lips twitched in a smile; he leaned forward, ready to engage with me.

Something gave way inside my chest, and I understood Shunji at last.

"We called it the forest of sincerity," I said in a bright tone. "I meant to say it was a *medieval* forest, but I got it wrong and the guys thought it was funny. But—"

"Nature good, big city bad, take a hike in the mountains and reconnect with your true self?" Murata-san said laconically.

"No. That forest... there's something *unnatural* about it. You have to fight it. Every minute you're in under those trees, you have to fight... there's something out there. Something *old*. You can *feel* it. Sometimes... We measured it. In certain places, within ten meters you can get a temperature variation of up to five degrees. That's in summer, OK? In winter it's actually worse. In winter, these places are *warm*. And... that's where we would find the bodies. Often it's one big tree that stands apart from the others. Or a clearing where a big tree fell. It's like these places *draw* them. You often find them at the end of the trails of suzuran tape."

I paused to evaluate Murata-san's reaction. He hadn't moved, but something sparkled on his temple. A drop of sweat had crawled out of his hair to glint in the sun. I smiled in satisfaction. He braced his hands on the floor as if to rise.

"Wait," I said. My face was probably doing more to scare him than my words, but I wanted him to have all the information he needed to support his decision to walk out of my life. If it was instinctive, he might later regret it. And the whole cycle might start all over again. "There's more."

There's some very weird kind of chain reaction going on in there, I told him. If a person heads out to Jukai to top themselves, they're not looking to mark their trail. Right? So we can take it that *they're* not responsible for the suzuran tape. It's like a fucking infestation, I told him. So who's stringing it up in there? Let's tentatively rule out the possibility that a supernatural entity is purchasing this stuff and whizzing about to knot it around the trees. Although I have to parenthetically tell you, I no longer think that's impossible. But the *likely* answer is: people like us. Hikers. Campers. Ghostbusters. Necrophilic heavy metal freaks out to get a personal eyeful of death. They string the stuff up and they don't bother to remove it when they leave. If they *do* leave – we found the bodies of quite a number of them. And so the poor fucking suicidal types, who are understandably in a state, looking for the easy route, and not exactly focused on their surroundings – they just automatically follow the suzuran tape. And when they reach the end of that particular trail, that seems to them like a natural stopping point, so they take their pills or they string up their own little pathetic bit of nylon rope.

Now let me get back to the common characteristics of these places where we found the bodies. The temperature tends to be different from the surrounding air. Clearings, I mentioned; also pits, depressions, and caves.

You can laugh at me if you like but I know there's something in there. It's under the ground. Think about it: that's the direction of hell.

Murata-san gulped visibly. The sweat had grown to a rainfall on his temples. He got out a handkerchief and mopped it away, all without taking his gaze off me.

There's SOMETHING in there, I relentlessly repeated. The lie of the land naturally attracts them to the places where it can come out and get them. And when they're dead, it goes on using them to attract more victims. Come on come on, little human beings, just follow the suzuran tape. *Sllss clitter rrrshhh.*

But now this chain reaction has taken off in a whole new way. And that's our fault.

Here's what happened. There was this guy, Areiya. He was just a regular guy. Long story short, he ended up in Jukai with a bottle of gin and a bottle of rat poison in his pockets. He reached the end of the suzuran tape and IT ME HIM WE took possession of his soul. And that's when Shunji and the others came tromping through the forest.

Anyone else would have left him the fuck alone. But not Shunji. Oh no, not my love. He ballsed right up to him, his heart singing with the thought that he had the chance to save a life.

Except it was already too late.

Now listen, I don't know the exact sequence of events. I do NOT know whether Areiya had drunk that rat poison yet. I don't think he had. But I think—

"I think," I finished softly, "that he was already dead."

Murata-san coughed several times and finally had to light a cigarette before he could speak. "Well," he said after a few puffs. "Not impossible."

"And now he's after me." I fingered my cross. "Next up is everyone I know." Did I have to spell it out for him?

Murata-san rarely smiled. Maybe he knew it made him look sad. He did now. "Well, I'd say he's picked the wrong target this time. Couple of outsiders." He gestured with his head at the CD rack, where the removal of Shunji's techno and trance discs had left my collection of heavy metal and hard rock leaning in tipsy piles. "We know all the vocabulary. If it's grotesque, we've thought of it already. No way he can knock us off balance..." He nodded, a touch too decisively. "He should have stuck to the easy marks."

"Shunji wasn't an easy mark," I said in honest outrage.

"Come on. All your friends. Privileged. Not saying they weren't good kids, but they never knew what it means to be exiled from society. They couldn't have been... ready. I am."

"Murata-san," I said. "Get out of here. Do you hear me? I wish I'd never said a word." I clenched my fists. "You still don't understand. You can't *imagine*. You're not ready and you never will be."

His smile drooped. "Been ready for years. Thought I'd die before I turned thirty. Now I'm just going through the motions, day in and day out: open the bar, play the music, count the money... Like floating in a vacuum. I'm ready."

"Fuck off," was all I could say, and it had the negative force of a formulaic lie.

The forest of sincerity. I should have remembered the kind of thing that starts to happen when you enter it and get lost.

"So," I said. I drank off the last of my coffee and rose on my heels. "At least I have an idea of *what* I'm dealing with. *How* to deal with it... well, I'll work that out. Maybe take a few CDs with me."

"How," Murata-san echoed. His big arms moved across the table to stack our empty plates. "I've never understood how people deal with this thing we call time."

"Me neither," I said. "But I know I don't have much of it." Given the speed at which Areiya had been recovering his strength after his fall, he'd be back on his feet within twenty-four hours. And if only for superstition's sake, I badly wanted to catch him while it was daylight.

I moved to the sliding doors and stared into the gloom of our bedroom. It already smelt like a single person's lonely lair. In the back of the closet was all our equipment: GPS, walkie-talkies, hiking boots, canteens, electronic compasses, neon vinyl tape to tie to trees, rope for emergencies, Swiss Army knives, spray paint, waterproof pouches for everything in case the rain came down again, leftover copies of the JuKyo flyers that we used to deposit about the forest in waterproof boxes (PLEASE DON'T COMMIT SUICIDE! THINK OF YOUR FAMILY!)... and suzuran tape. No need for that, this time around. On the other hand, I would be adding some crucial items to the kit: the longest knife in the kitchen and the airgun that Maedaza had once given me as a birthday present.

But whatever I chose to take with me, it would be a fine

balancing act between preparedness and maneuverability, and I needed to be alone to get it right. I cracked the doors, hoping Murata-san would take the hint.

I heard him lumbering to his feet. "Coming with you," he said.

Keeping my back to him, I said, "No."

Clumsily, he touched my shoulder. "Make a couple of phone calls." He mentioned the names of a couple of our regulars, a musician and a professional pachinko player who probably hadn't seen daylight in the last ten years. "Backup."

And I could see it all happening again. Vividly, I saw Shunji's face in my mind — *If I'd known how it was going to end, I'd never have involved you, BELIEVE ME!*

But we never do know how it's going to end, do we? That's the hell of this thing called time.

I smiled at Murata-san and said, "Think either of them owns a pair of hiking boots?"

About the Author

Felicity Savage is a major award-nominated fantasy author. MUSIC TO DIE BY is her first suspense novel. Born in South Carolina, Savage lived until the age of two in rural France, and then in the west of Ireland. At six, she moved with her family to the island of North Uist in the Outer Hebrides, where she joined the Girl Guides and appeared in productions of Robin Hood and Peter Pan at the RAF base on Benbecula. Some years later she graduated from Columbia College in New York City and then moved to Japan, where she now lives with her husband, daughter, and two cats. When not writing, she works as a Japanese translator, sings Gregorian chant, and moonlights as a serial houseplant killer.

Visit the author at http://felicitysavage.com/

Exclusive Extra!

If you enjoyed this book, read on for a sneak preview of Felicity Savage's first suspense novel, now available from Knights Hill Publishing.

Music to Die By

a suspense novel by

Felicity Savage

A singer in Tokyo's scuzzy indie rock scene, Shanti Hazard buried her past long ago. But when childhood friend Ned turns up in the audience at one of her band's shows, he threatens to reveal the ugly secret he and Shanti share.

Determined to protect her friends and bandmates, Shanti plots to outwit Ned while the band tours snowbound Japan, sleeping on couches. A botched cover-up leads to murder and a tightening web of deception, as the band clashes with the merciless Japanese legal system.

Ultimately, to defeat her past, Shanti will have to confront it… and Ned… before someone else dies.

Music to Die By plunges the reader into the gritty world of the Japanese indie rock scene, building to a shocking climax. The first suspense novel from acclaimed fantasy author Felicity Savage, *Music to Die By* is now available from Knights Hill Publishing in print and ebook editions.

Excerpt follows…

Felicity Savage

Music to Die By

Part I: Unfair Game

"**L**et's talk about you," I snarled. "It must've been the first time. So did it excite you?"

Gen stood on my left, hunched over his Ibanez as if he were trying to protect it from the crowd. He wore his uniform of jeans and a plain black t-shirt. Sweat fell sparkling from his curls. When I tore into the chorus, he raised his head and bellowed the harmony into his own mic. He had the best voice of any of the boys, a raspy tenor that harmonized nicely with my own voice. I was more of a shouter than a singer, and inevitably got Janis Joplin comparisons, although I preferred to think of myself as the female Layne Staley, without the heroin problem. I had enough problems as it was.

Our faithful supporters swayed an arm's length in front of me, chaotically out of step. About three-quarters of our guest list had showed up by the time we went on stage. It does mean something to be headlining. And it didn't hurt, either, that Ace's High was so small that this modest crowd was a capacity one. We couldn't take all the credit: Dew Over, Bloodthirsty Fakers, and Vanilla Camp had left a residue of punters who were determined to get full value for money, curious about a band with two gaijins in it, or simply willing to give us a try. Some of them had trickled away during our first number, but others lingered. They even clapped.

Unlike Gen, I didn't just stand there. I covered the whole stage – which wasn't difficult: I could only take two paces before I bumped into Gen or Tad, our bassist. I struck poses, touched myself, danced with the mic stand, and interacted with the boys. My bottle-green top hat shadowed my face in the hot, shifting spotlights. When I finally doffed it, applause went up. I mugged, did a clownish shuffle, then hooked the hat on my mic stand and started dancing in earnest. I wore my cowboy boots, my lucky talismans, harness brown with turquoise, gold, and white flames. Their heels made me tall enough to see four or five deep into the crowd.

"Let's talk about you," I ranted, "and the little places you call home."

Tad planted his left foot on a wedge speaker and banged his head as he churned out the bass solo. A pair of black cat ears poked out of his flying hair. At home he also had floppy white bunny ears, tall grey donkey ears, and a magician's hat with stars and moons on it. He liked to wear that one with a gold kimono.

"It was the only thing you've ever done! I hope, oh yeah, I hope it was a good one."

I extended the end of the phrase into a melodic scream, jammed my mic onto the stand, and let my head fall forward as Gen took over for the outro. Through the curtain of hair that slid in front of my face, I saw constellations of cigarette ends explode in the outer darkness as the technique freaks applauded. I straightened up and gestured broadly, helping the spotlight on Gen to make its point.

Joaquin crashed both hands down on the keyboard of his Korg. An instant of silence, and then the applause kicked in. I stepped back to the mic and thanked the crowd.

"For those of you that we haven't got to know yet, Joaquin's the tunesmith." In his place behind the Korg, Joaquin bowed. "I write the lyrics. They let me do that because I can't play an instrument."

Tad grabbed my mic and said, "I've got an idea, Shanti. You can have my job and I'll have yours."

I grinned and said over the catcalls, "Shut up, Tad, I'm busy showing off my Japanese."

This got a huge laugh, as usual. To the extent I spoke

Japanese, I spoke it like a native. For that I could thank my sense of pitch, but more to the point, as Joaquin could have explained, once you have a second language, it's no big deal to acquire a third one. As a kid in Paris, I'd gone from zero to fluent in French in a year, and as an adult in Tokyo, it had taken me only slightly longer than that to learn Japanese. I still had plenty of holes in my vocabulary, but they didn't show onstage.

"Now guess what, you lucky people, we're going to do a song off the new album. U-Turn Day, out next Saturday from Cold Coeur Records. Available from your local clued-up independent music store, or buy it on our website, where we're streaming select tracks for your listening pleasure. Now here's another dirty little sample." I leaned into the mic. "When I first started writing lyrics for Gorot, I didn't want to write about the same old thing. You know. Lurrrve."

Nina, Joaquin's wife and our recording angel, dodged across the Bermuda Crescent in front of the stage with her digital camera. Our Shimokitazawa gigs rarely got rowdy enough for the crowd to venture into that buffer zone between us and them. Even when they did, they retreated when the music stopped.

"But I've learned a lot since I've been in this band," I said. "I've realized that I have more to say about life in general than I ever knew."

I saw him.

His blond hair shone in the dark. He was leaning against the wall about three people behind Nina. At this distance I couldn't see his eyes.

"A lot to say," I repeated. "A lot to say."

I had nothing to say to Ned Gallant, now or ever.

But maybe it wasn't him. Maybe it was just some coworker of Nina's who hadn't been on the guest list, or one of the European drifters Joaquin collected.

Tad glanced sharply at me. I couldn't tell if he was alarmed, or just trying to prompt me, but it reminded me why I was here, why I'd written the song I was currently supposed to be introducing, and how I'd felt while I was writing it, in my tiny studio apartment with my headphones on, pushing rewind over and over again on the rough mix: as far from Ireland as I would ever get.

"Recently," I said, "I realized that I even have something to say about love. And this is it. 'Heartbreak.'"

I signaled to Joaquin with one hand behind my back. The silence lengthened: one, two, three, and the first plaintive piano notes floated out over Tad's bass line. Shingo tapped on the rim of the snare, a sinister rhythm like a clock ticking. Until its closing seconds, this song required no more of Gen than filler duties. "Heartbreak" was that rare thing in our repertoire, a slow burner designed to prove that I could actually sing, and that was appropriate, because it was my song of liberation.

"Struck dumb by a closing door," I sang, cupping my mic in both hands for a bit of distortion, "face down on the bathroom floor. Here's a dirty little sample, better keep it to yourself. I've lived, I've been, I've seen…"

Joaquin's line swelled, surging towards maximum volume.

"I've sunk, I've swum, I've fallen in between…"

Someone whistled deafeningly.

"And you, you think that you'll remain in my memory like a stain, but you'll fade like everyone! You were never here!"

Sweet, languid Jonathan had been the lead guitarist of the first band I was ever in, back in New York, and I'd thought he was the love of my life, until he turned out to be a cheater and a liar. When he cheated on me, I hadn't just dumped him, I'd left the country. Top that, asshole. I'd won, but it had taken me another four years to write him, literally, out of my heart.

And in the meantime, I'd discovered something strange and surprising, better than sex and almost as good as music.

Friendship.

I'd once had a boyfriend. Now I had four boy friends

who meant more to me than Jonathan ever had.

I'd written "Heartbreak" for them, and if the lyrics didn't really reflect that… well, my lyrics always turned out kind of dark.

I couldn't lose them. I couldn't, but my own words sounded like a dire prophecy as I sobbed, "Stupid enough to not quite see the temporary nature of everything behind your eyes!"

It was Gen's moment. Unexpectedly, he launched a gargoyle of a riff that climbed on the back of Joaquin's piano line and reached for the stratosphere. We'd heard this variation in rehearsal, but never live. I signaled to Tad and went for a repeat of the chorus. Gen's riff toyed with my voice, then folded up and flatlined into a distorted hum that grew louder and louder until it swallowed Joaquin's last notes.

After that, our last number was an anticlimax. I thrashed around the stage, but I couldn't stop looking at that spot over by the wall. In a montage of underexposed stills, I saw him draining a can of beer, taking off his knit cap, and putting two fingers in his mouth and whistling. So it had been him.

"Encore! Encore!"

For once I wished our supporters weren't quite so faithful.

"Encore!"

I bowed for the third time. Behind me, Joaquin hissed, "What are you waiting for?"

"No encore," I said through my smile.

"Fuck off. What's wrong?"

With the show officially over, we could take a minute to confer. I went back to Joaquin, mic in hand. His face was scarlet and his hands hovered on the keyboard. "OK," I told him, "I'll do an encore. But not 'You're No Fun.'"

"Don't give me this shit. If you don't want to do it, why did you want it on the set list?"

"Joaquin, I can't fucking do it!"

Joaquin's jaw tightened. He seized the mic from my hand and plunged around the Korg, shaking the cord clear.

"OK, we'll do another track from Xenophobia," he said out of the side of his mouth. "They've heard the whole album many times, but what the hell."

He arrived at the front of the stage in a single stride with his smile on full. A storm of clapping greeted him. Everyone knew he was the brains of the band, and although he seldom took a producer's bow, they felt he deserved it. He thanked them in English, Japanese, and French, and waited for the applause to subside. I hovered at his side, trying to look supportive rather than apprehensive. He said in Japanese, "We are delighted that you come all the way to Shimokitazawa to see us. I mean, it's the middle of nowhere, eh?"

Laughter.

"We hope you will come all the way to Hokkaido to see us, too! We can't reimburse you for the airfare, but we think it will be worth it. They say that Sapporo is a beautiful city. Myself, I've never been there, but I'm looking forward to it. Yes, ladies and gentlemen, Gorot is going on tour!"

I did what I had to do, which was lead the applause. When we were debating whether to tour for U-Turn Day, I'd been anti. I didn't know why I even bothered, since Joaquin always got his way in the end.

"Some of you are familiar with Kinderbox," continued Joaquin, naming another of the acts he produced for our label, Cold Coeur Records, which he also owned. "We tour together. We will look for you next week in Sapporo! Hakodate! Aomori! Morioka! Yamagata! Sendai! Fukushima! And Utsunomiya! But if we don't see you there, we hope to meet on Tuesday the twelfth of March at Oasis in Shinjuku, where we plan a party for our homecoming. It is also the release party for U-Turn Day! Yoroshiku onegai shimasu. Also," Joaquin added rapidly, "we have gigs upcoming throughout March, please check out the information on the flyers. We're running late, but we will do one more song for you tonight. 'Dreamstomper.'" Throwing me a look of triumph mixed with a challenge, he hopped back behind the Korg.

Numbly, I waited for the piano loop to roll out of the speakers. In the interval of rustling silence I cleared my throat. "This one's for everyone who got lost along the way," I said, wishing Ned Gallant had.

Backstage, Nina handed out bottles of Crystal Geyser. Joaquin upended his over his head, splashing everyone. "To Cold Coeur Family Volume I!" This, unbelievably, was what our tour had come to be called. Infected by his mood, the other boys slavishly acted like they'd all been excited about it from the start. The manager played along, too, opining that it would be just the ticket to launch us into the big time. Joaquin followed him into his office to sort out our cut of the door. After retrieving our kit from the stage, Gen, Tad, and Shingo piled into the cruddy little restroom down the hall and jostled for access to the tap.

I gulped water. As soon as Joaquin squared the manager, we were due to join up with our faithful supporters and head to an izakaya. Ned might turn out to be someone else, and it wouldn't be the first time. My fight-or-flight reflex often went off at the sight of a blond head and a pair of blue eyes. But if it had been him...

Pushing a hand through my damp, tangled hair, I went out the side door and said hello to my friends. There were about two dozen people left in the house, and I didn't know all their faces, let alone their names. Back in Gorot's early days, the same people had come to all our gigs and we'd gone to all their gigs; now we had friends and fans, and it was getting harder to tell which were which. I clocked the blond guy hovering near the exit.

I went back through the grey room, past the manager's office and the restroom, looking for another way out. There was an emergency exit, but it was padlocked.

I retrieved my shoulderbag, threw on my coat, and ducked back through the side door. I didn't have a plan. All I knew was that I had to keep Ned away from the band. I couldn't be sure that he wouldn't approach me in front of them, and I was even less sure of my own ability to deny to his face that we'd ever met. I wasn't even sure that would be the best line to take. He might react unpredictably.

"Shanti, you're not skipping out?" Nina said in astonishment.

"You're on PR duty, gorgeous," I said. "Oh, I left my hatbox back there. Could you take it home with you? I'll come over and pick it up tomorrow or sometime."

I beelined to the exit, calling goodnight to the technicians who were shutting down the equipment onstage. As I passed the blond guy, he took an abortive step towards me. I pushed through the door into February. His footsteps echoed mine on the stairs. Out on the street, the rest of our supporters were hanging around in groups, smoking and chatting. I shouted to them that I had an early start tomorrow and inconsistently turned left, away from the station. He caught up with me. I kept walking. At the 7-11 on the corner I turned again. He matched my strides. A cold, dusty wind blew around us.

"Fuck, this feels weird." His voice was deep. I'd subconsciously been expecting him to sound like a child. "But it feels kind of natural, too, doesn't it?"

"Well, it's been a while," I said, head ringing.

"A while?" He laughed. He looked like none of the men I'd mistaken for him over the years. He was still blond, and his eyes were still that eerie blue – but he was no longer small or pale or skinny. His skin had seen a lot of sun, and he hulked over me with shoulders as broad as the axle of a small car. He'd turned out as big as Nigel. But his accent no longer sounded like Nigel's. It had softened dramatically. "I guess you've added the art of understatement to your repertoire. It's been half our lives. No, more. I was twelve, and your birthday is before mine, so you'd have been thirteen."

He spoke as if he didn't remember exactly. This confused me.

"So how's Alastair doing these days?"

We were turning corners at random, and although I couldn't remember crossing the railway tracks, we must have done, because we were now descending the gentle hill on the far side of Shimokitazawa station. Shuttered boutiques lined the narrow street. Here and there, golden light from the windows of a restaurant shone through a screen of trees. The wind numbed my face; it seemed to have penetrated to my bones and slowed down my brain. Ned and I were talking. How had this happened?

"Alastair lives in the States," I said. My brother had spent his early twenties trying to be an artist; now he was the assistant manager of Windrose & Sons, a 150-year-old gallery in Boston's Back Bay that sold objets d'art and antiques from all over the world, true to its origins as a clearing-house for plunder from the Orient. He and his girlfriend Maisie lived together in Somerville with her second-hand Volvo, his BMW 6-series, and two Weimaraners, and he seemed happy. "He's doing OK, I guess."

"Figures. He was bound to land on his feet. And June? Still painting, is she?"

"She moved back to France years ago," I said. Our mother had nothing to do with it. Ned would have no reason to track her down, nor could he learn anything from her he didn't already know. "She lives near Bordeaux now. It's la France profonde, the true France. She keeps chickens and goats. And yeah, she's still painting her heart out."

Ned laughed. "You know something funny? All this time I thought your family was still in Thailand."

"You're kidding! We only stayed there for six months."

I remembered promising Ned that he could come with us. Promising it would be all right. But I was only thirteen and it wasn't my decision to make.

Ned would probably have hated Thailand, though. We did. After Ireland, it had been so hot that I felt like I'd stepped onto another planet. I remembered the energy draining from my thirteen-year-old body, the sunlight so bright that my eyes hurt, and a hundred and one permutations of

136

boredom and anxiety. That was nothing to how June must have felt. She'd dragged us halfway around the world to the one man who had to take us in: our father. Malcolm Ogilvie had settled in Phuket. He was a poet – we'd owned an actual book of poetry by him at one point – but he subsisted on the generosity of hotel and bar managers who gave him odd jobs. From his point of view, having the three of us descend on him must have been the worst trip of his life, especially since he had a live-in Thai girlfriend.

Somehow, we all managed to cohabit in his disgusting bungalow for five or six months. That was how long it took June to accept that she'd made a mistake. She fell back on her brother Red, my corporate lawyer uncle in Philadelphia. And just like that, as if the first thirteen years of my life had been a dream, I'd suddenly had the life of a privileged American teenager.

Not for long, though. Unlike Alastair, I hadn't been able to keep it up.

"As for our father," I said, "he's dead."

It was Ned's turn to exclaim, "You're kidding!" And in his smile I saw a hint of schadenfreude that chilled me to the bone.

"He hanged himself about ten years ago," according to the letter that the Thai girlfriend had sent June. It had been wrapped around a small teak box that contained Malcolm's ashes. "He left a typical, self-pitying note. Saying he'd failed everyone and he was sorry. Talk about wasted sentiments. *We* weren't."

Ned hissed between his teeth. I thought I'd succeeded in shocking him. But he said in the same easy tone as before, "Funny thing is, *I* live in Thailand now. On Koh Samui. I go across to Phuket all the time, and I used to ask around for you, but no one's ever heard of you or your father."

Shit.

"Ned, how on earth did you end up in Thailand?"

"I'm an architect," he said, and went on expansively, in the strange nonaccent he'd acquired. "Koh Samui is booming.

The tsunami created a lot of opportunities. New regulations, new land up for sale. I've got my own business, building villas. Referrals from all over. The clients appreciate having someone on the ground to see their projects through to completion: they don't want to deal with the Thais themselves. They're racist fuckers, as a rule. But I believe in doing the best work possible."

"Wow."

"I'm building my own house, too. It's still under construction. I've been working on it on and off for the last four years. But it's going to be fucking stunning. I can show you some photos if you're interested."

Laughter bubbled up in my chest. Ned was a *builder*. I didn't know why this struck me as so funny. I said, "Cool. Did you study architecture at school?" I wanted to find out where he'd spent the twelve years that were still unaccounted for. Why couldn't I just ask?

"Sure, I learned on the job. That's the best way. Hands-on experience. You've got to be focused, though. Thailand is full of Westerners who just drift from beach to beach..." Ned shook his head.

"Oh, we've got them here, too, except they don't come for the beaches. They come for the jobs."

"Still, I can't criticize that lifestyle. I lived on Bali for a while. Bummed around Indonesia, Malaysia, India." We reached the level crossing at the bottom of the hill. The barrier was down, the warning bell pinging. "I guess I was looking for something, but I didn't know what it was," Ned shouted as a train rushed past. "Maybe it was just a decent living," he added, laughing.

"Look," I said, pointing to a record shop on a side street. "They sell our albums. We've got our own label, and we're hooked up with an independent distributor."

"Oh yeah? Way to go!"

"Jesus, Ned, what *has* happened to your accent? You sound almost American."

"You sound fairly American yourself, Shanti."

"Well, I went to school on the East Coast. High school in Philly, and then NYU." No need to mention that I hadn't graduated, committing myself to rock 'n' roll instead of to the library.

"Get a load of you. I didn't go to university at all. After you left, my grandmother showed up and took me back to Denmark with her."

"Denmark!" That was it, of course. He didn't sound American. He sounded ever so slightly Scandinavian. The legend came back to me all at once: the mother who did a runner when Ned was three, leaving Nigel to raise him whilst making a go of his business, Allihies Ceramics. I even remembered Ned telling me where she'd come from. Somewhere like Norway, but without the funky mythic associations. *Denmark.* "I didn't know you even *had* a grandmother!" I said.

"Neither did I, until she walked in and told me to pack my stuff. I had a terrible time adjusting in Copenhagen. Couldn't get my tongue around the language. I used to think about you and Alastair jabbering away to each other in French. How did you do it? I picked up enough Danish in the end to get by, but as soon as I got out of school I buggered off. I used to go back as often as possible to see my grandmother, though. I owed her, didn't I?"

"She must be an amazing lady," to have put up with you, I added to myself.

"She was. She died last year."

"Oh Ned, I'm so sorry."

I caught his flickering glance of contempt. He didn't believe I was sorry, although when I said it, I *had* been.

We rounded the corner onto the plaza. I veered towards the station entrance and started up the stairs. Ned climbed beside me. He was explaining how it was that he could jaunt off to Japan at his pleasure, with zero hardship or sacrifice, but I wasn't really listening, because I knew it was just a bunch of excuses. I was wondering if I could lose him in Tokyo's fiendishly complicated rail system. "Have you got a ticket?"

"I need to buy one, do I? Where to?"

I thought quickly. "To Shibuya, but the tickets are priced by distance. It's a hundred and twenty yen."

I watched him shoulder through the milling crowd to the ticket machines, scoop change out of his pocket, and examine every coin before putting one into the slot. I had a prepaid Passnet card. I thought about dashing through the wickets while his back was turned. But there was only one platform. I'd have much better odds of losing him in Shibuya, where the JR, Tokyu, and Keio Inogashira train lines and the Ginza, Hanzomon, and Denentoshi subway lines all looped around each other in a multistorey knot.

As we came out of the wickets at Shibuya, I plunged ahead of Ned into the horde pouring down into the Mark City building. He seized the shoulder strap of my bag. "You don't mind if I hang onto you? This is fucking mad. I've never seen anything like it in my life. Feel like I'm about to be swept off my feet."

"Yeah, it's crazy, isn't it," I said, teeth gritted in frustration.

But then again, if I'd cut and run I would have looked guilty. And he'd just turn up again at our next gig, wouldn't he? My only hope was to brazen it out and get rid of him by some means as yet beyond the reach of my imagination. Leave him as completely as possible in the dark.

Yet every minute he was finding out more about my new life. I showed him how to buy a JR ticket and we rode the Yamanote line south, squashed shoulder to shoulder between drowsy drunks and noisy ones. At Gotanda I got off. He got off. We left the station and walked along a dark street, embroidered on one side with snack bar signs, which led back along the foot of the Yamanote line embankment. There was no traffic. Gotanda was an undercover town, buttoned up during the day and sleazy by night, with the highest concentration of love hotels south of Shibuya. You never bumped into anyone you knew here, which was why it suited me.

Among the office buildings on this side of the station towered a few elderly apartment blocks. I came to the dinged elevator doors at the foot of my building and turned to face Ned, feeling panicky. "Well, now you know where I live."

"Pretty ritzy." He craned his neck to look up at eight floors of concrete balconies.

"At least it's supposed to be earthquake-proof," I said.

"Oh sure, that would be a concern in this country."

We stood between the morgue-like walls of mailboxes. Was he waiting for me to invite him in? Did he plan on crashing *at my place?* No. No. No. This was not happening.

"Whereabouts are you staying, Ned?" I said bluntly.

"I've a couple of mates living in the city." He looked away from me. There was a trace of anger in his voice. "They came to Japan to work and save money, and they're spending it as fast as they make it, but they're good lads. I'll introduce you at some point. Mike's got a job in the public school system; Gavin works for one of these English conversation schools, same as you. They're raking it in. So they've a house, not just a crappy little apartment, in Nakano. You know where that is?"

Five minutes west on the Chuo line from Shinjuku. A goodly haul from here. But nowhere would be far enough.

"I can stay with them as long as I want. It's party central, but I'm not fussy. You've no need to worry about me on that score!" Ned chuckled, an unamused masculine sound that reminded me of Nigel.

"Ned, how did you find me?" I blurted. Immediately, I had a sensation of having taken a misstep. "I've often thought about *you*, but I had no way of knowing where you were."

He looked at me for a long minute. I concentrated on not letting a muscle of my face twitch. At last he said, "I searched for your name on the internet. Googled you, and up you popped. Your band's website. Pictures and everything."

I'd known it. I'd *known* it.

"So I knew it was you. Of course, it had to be you; there can't be two people in the world named Shanti Hazard."

Oh God. To hell with staying true to myself. I should have changed my name.

"That was about eighteen months ago."

So I'd been living in jeopardy, my illusion of safety hanging by a thread, for more than a year.

But how could I have talked the boys out of putting up a website? How could I have forced them to leave me off it? I was the face of Gorot, literally – Tad had used a picture of me for our logo, and they were always pushing for more pictures: pictures of me walking on the beach, drinking coffee, laughing out loud – pictures that would make me seem like someone you knew. I vetoed all but the blurriest live shots. That had made me feel better about the website, as did the fact that not much of the information on it was in English. But what difference did that make when my *name* was out there?

"I thought about getting in touch there and then, but you know how it is. Life gets in the way. By the time I finally got around to it, I thought I might as well just pop over and see you. So I got a Japanese mate to translate the squiggly bits for me, and here I am!"

"And how do you like it so far?" I keened softly through my chattering teeth.

"Well, I'll tell you. It's bloody confusing and it's bloody cold." Ned lowered his voice conspiratorially. "And do you get the feeling that these people don't know how to relax? This is according to my Japanese mate at home, but the culture here is fucking totalitarian. The level of social control is such that the people can't make their own choices. If they could, maybe they'd choose to be a bit more free!"

"I like it here because I fit in," I said, provoking a cry of disbelief from him. I explained, though it felt futile: "I didn't do very well as an American. It's much easier to be a foreigner."

"Well, in that case, then, I know what you mean! It was a

142

nightmare living in Denmark, as I said. Looking like them but not speaking their language, not knowing their TV shows or their songs, not knowing shit about their fucking history and not caring. But when you're a Westerner out East, no one cares where you supposedly come from. No one asks why you've got a funny accent. You don't have to pretend to be something you're not. You can be yourself, can't you?"

Ned's face lit up as the words tumbled out. I didn't want to agree with him about anything, so I said nothing.

"Shanti, this is the kind of conversation I want to have with you! It's not everyone who understands, is it? But you're on my wavelength. You've had the same life experiences. You were *there.*"

Feeling dizzy, I steadied myself on the mailboxes.

"I just want to talk. No games, no bullshit." He looked eagerly into my face. "I just want us to be open with each other."

"Yeah, OK," I said faintly, "but can we do it some other time? I'm dead on my feet, and if I don't get indoors, I'm going to die of hypothermia."

"Oh well, then, I won't keep you," he said, drawing back with unsettling rapidity. "We couldn't have *that*, could we?"

END OF EXCERPT

Music to Die By is now available for purchase from your preferred online book retailer in print and ebook editions. Learn more about the book and the author at http://felicitysavage.com/